"I'll give you some advice, Stella— sometimes there's such a thing as caring too much."

At that, she looked back at him. And he'd been right. There were tears in her eyes. He had to stop himself before he reached for her, because really, she was a stranger to him. He didn't know her anymore, and he didn't care to know her. He was only here for a business deal.

"For me, as far as Frances is concerned, there is no such thing as caring too much."

He wondered how it was that they'd ended up so differently. Her caring too much, and him not caring at all. They were two stars at the opposite ends of the universe. And she still shone just as brightly as she had when she was fourteen. Maybe he was jealous of that. Deep down. Maybe he wanted to love just as fiercely as Stella Clarke did.

She lifted her chin. "You can take your money, and your offer, and go to hell, Ian," she said.

And walked out.

Dear Reader,

It's the holiday season in Christmas Bay—wreaths are hanging on the old-fashioned street lamps, shoppers are strolling down frosty Main Street and the Christmas countdown has officially begun. It's a time for family, love, peace and forgiveness. But for Stella Clarke and Ian Steele, it's going to take more than holiday magic to help tear down the walls that have kept them apart their entire lives. It's going to take a leap of faith that will finally allow them to trust again and, more than that, to fall in love.

I hope that Stella and Ian's story, *Their Christmas Resolution*, will make you believe in happy endings, and that the sparkle of the Christmas season, and of our little town on the coast, will stay with you all year long.

Kaylie Newell

Their Christmas Resolution

—

KAYLIE NEWELL

HARLEQUIN
SPECIAL
EDITION

HARLEQUIN®
SPECIAL EDITION™

Recycling programs
for this product may
not exist in your area.

ISBN-13: 978-1-335-59431-0

Their Christmas Resolution

Copyright © 2023 by Kaylie Newell

For questions and comments about the quality of this book, please contact us at CustomerService@Harlequin.com.

Harlequin Enterprises ULC
22 Adelaide St. West, 41st Floor
Toronto, Ontario M5H 4E3, Canada
www.Harlequin.com

Printed in U.S.A.

For **Kaylie Newell**, storytelling is in the blood. Growing up the daughter of two writers, she knew eventually she'd want to follow in their footsteps. She's now the proud author of over twenty books, including the RITA® Award finalists *Christmas at the Graff* and *Tanner's Promise*.

Kaylie lives in Southern Oregon with her husband, two daughters, a blind Doberman and two indifferent cats. Visit Kaylie at Facebook.com/kaylienewell.

Books by Kaylie Newell

Harlequin Special Edition

Sisters of Christmas Bay

Their Sweet Coastal Reunion
Their All-Star Summer

Visit the Author Profile page
at Harlequin.com for more titles.

For Amy and Nola, my Christmas angels.

Chapter One

Ian Steele leaned back in his full grain leather chair, the one he'd just dropped three grand on, and looked out at the sparkling waters of San Francisco Bay. The light in his office this time of day was soft, golden. The sun filtered in through the blinds in warm rays, making the dust particles in the air look like stars. He'd always liked San Francisco this time of year. It was almost Christmas, but it didn't necessarily feel *Christmassy*, which suited him just fine. He could almost look out the window at the sailboats bouncing over the swells and mistake it for summertime.

There was a soft knock on his door, but he didn't take his eyes off the view below. "Come in," he said evenly.

"Ian, there's a call for you on line one."

At the sound of Jill's voice, he swiveled around to see her standing with her hands clasped in front of her stomach. She always looked apologetic these days, like she didn't want to upset him. He could be an ass, but she was the consummate professional, which was why he'd hired her in the first place.

He smiled, trying his best to put her at ease. But truth be told, he'd probably have a better shot at swimming across the bay without being eaten by a shark. She had the distinct look of someone standing on broken glass.

"Who is it?" he asked.

"Stella Clarke. Says she's from Christmas Bay." She frowned. "Where's that?"

Ian stiffened. It had been years since he'd thought of his hometown. Maybe even longer since he'd heard anyone mention Christmas Bay. He'd cut that part of his life out as neatly as a surgeon. He was too busy now, too successful to spend much time dwelling on things like his childhood, which quite frankly didn't deserve a single minute of reflection.

"Tiny little town on the Oregon Coast." He rubbed his jaw. "What the hell does she want, anyway?"

His assistant's eyebrows rose at this. Clearly, she was taken aback. Ian was usually smooth as scotch. Unruffled by much of anything.

Clearing his throat, he leaned back in his brand-new chair. He had the ridiculous urge to loosen his tie, but resisted out of sheer willpower. "Did she say? What she wants?"

"She has a favor to ask. She said she knows you're busy but that it won't take much time."

Typical Stella. Exactly how he remembered her. He could see her standing in the living room on the day he'd arrived at the foster home, when his heart had been the heaviest, and his anger the sharpest. Wild, dark hair. Deep blue eyes. Even at fourteen years old, she'd been a force to be reckoned with. Even with all she'd probably endured. Just like him. Just like all of them. She'd been whip-smart, direct, always trying to negotiate something for her benefit.

But he couldn't exactly talk. Now he made a living out of negotiating things for his own benefit. A very nice living, as a matter of fact. As one of the Bay Area's top real estate developers, he'd been snatching up prime property for years, building on it and then selling it for loads of cash. He had people standing in line to do his bidding. The question was, what was this favor she was talking about? And how much time would it actually take?

He looked at his Apple Watch, the cool metal band glinting in the sunlight. Almost noon. He had a meeting across town at two thirty, and he hadn't eaten yet. He could have Jill take her number, and he could call her back. Or not. But for some damn reason, he was curious about what she wanted. And whether he'd admit it or not, he was itching to hear her voice again. A voice that would now be seasoned by age, but would no doubt still be as soft as velvet. He hadn't talked to her since he'd graduated from Portland State. They'd run into each other at a swanky restaurant in the city where she'd been a server. They'd awkwardly met for coffee after the place closed, and it hadn't gone well. At all.

"Thanks, Jill," he said. "I'll take it. Have a good lunch."

She smoothed her hands down the front of her cream-colored pencil skirt. "Do you want me to bring you something back?"

He smiled again. "No. Thank you, though. Why don't you take an extra half hour? Get some time outside if you can. You've been working hard this morning, and the weather's nice. Enjoy it."

"Are you sure?"

"Positive. Go."

She reached for the door and pulled it closed behind her.

He looked down at the blinking button on the sleek black phone and felt his heart beat in time with it.

Picking it up, he stabbed the button with his index finger.

"Ian Steele," he said in a clipped tone.

"Ian? It's Stella Clarke. From Christmas Bay..."

He let out an even breath he hadn't realized he'd been holding. He'd been right. Her voice was still soft as velvet.

"Stella."

He waited, imagining what she might look like on the other end of the line. Wondering if that voice matched the rest of her. If she was that different than she'd been ten years ago. Because back then, the last time he'd seen her, she'd been very beautiful, and very pissed.

At least, she'd been pissed with him.

There was a long pause, and she cleared her throat. "How have you been?" she asked.

She was obviously trying to be polite, but he didn't give a crap about that right about now. He had things to do, and opening a window into the past was definitely not one of them.

"What do you want, Stella?"

"Well, it's nice to talk to you, too."

"I know you didn't call for a trip down memory lane."

"I took a chance that you might care about what's happening here," she said evenly. "Even if it's just a little."

"Why would I care about Christmas Bay?" He had no idea if that sounded convincing or not. Because he thought there might be an edge to his voice that said he did care, just the tiniest bit. Even if it was just being curious as to why she was calling after all this time. Curiosity he could live with. Caring, he couldn't. At least not about that Podunk little town.

"Because you have memories here, Ian."

He shook his head. *Unbelievable.* Of course she'd assume his memories at Frances's house were good ones. Worth keeping, if only in the corner of his mind.

The thing was, though, she was actually right. Not that he'd ever admit it. There were some good memories. Of course there were. Of Stella, whom he'd always gravitated toward, despite her sometimes-prickly ways. She was a survivor, and he'd admired that. She was a leader and a nurturer, and he'd admired that, too. He'd seen in her things he wished he'd seen in himself growing up. Things he'd had to teach himself as he'd gotten older, or at least fake.

And there were other memories that weren't so terrible. Memories of Frances. Of his aunt. And snippets of things, soft things, that he'd practically let slip away over the years, because they'd been intermingled with the bad stuff, and tarnished by time.

He gripped the phone tighter, until he felt it grow slick with perspiration. Those decent memories were the only reason he hadn't hung up on her by now. Those, and his ever-present curiosity.

"What do you want, Stella?" he repeated.

And this time, the question was sincere.

"I can't believe I just did that," Stella muttered under her breath.

Sinking down in her favorite chair in the sunroom, she looked over at Frances, who was wearing another one of her bedazzled Christmas sweaters.

Her fat black-and-white cat was curled up on her lap, purring like someone with a snoring problem.

"Uh-oh," Frances said, stroking Beauregard's head. "What?"

Stella worried her bottom lip with her teeth, and gazed out the window to the Pacific Ocean. It was misty today. Cold. But still stunningly beautiful— the ocean a deep, churning blue-gray below the dramatic cliffs where the house hovered. One of the loveliest houses in Christmas Bay. But of course, she was biased.

She'd moved in when she was a preteen and brand new to the foster system. At the time, she'd thought Frances's two-hundred-year-old Victorian was the only good thing about her unbelievably crappy situation. After all, it was rumored to be haunted, and how cool was that? But she'd also been a young girl at the time, and incredibly naive. She had no way of knowing that Frances herself would end up being the best thing about her situation. Frances and the girls who became not only her foster sisters, but her sisters of the heart. Getting to live in the house had been a bonus.

Now, as the thought of selling it crept back in, along with the thought of Frances's Alzheimer's diagnosis, which had changed things dramatically over the last few years, Stella felt a lump rise in her throat.

Swallowing it back down again, she forced a smile. This was going to be hard enough on her foster mother without her falling apart. Selling was the right thing to do. They just had to find the right buyer, that was all. Frances's only caveat was that a family needed to live here. A family who would love it as much as her own family had. As much as all of her foster kids had over the years.

"I asked someone for a favor," she said. "And now I'm wishing I hadn't."

"Why?"

She took a deep breath. "Since *Coastal Monthly* is doing that Christmas article on the house, I thought it would be a great time to kill two birds with one stone. Drum up some interest from potential buyers, and get the locals to stop telling that old ghost story."

Frances leaned forward, eliciting a grunt from Beauregard. "What do you mean? How in the world would you do that?"

It had been a long time. Almost fifteen years. Frances might have Alzheimer's, but her long-term memory was just fine. Stella wasn't sure how she'd react to this next piece of information. Maybe she'd be okay with it. But maybe not.

She braced herself, hoping for the former. "I called Ian Steele…"

Her foster mother's blue eyes widened. She sat there for minute, and Stella could hear the grandfather clock in the living room ticking off the seconds.

"Wow," Frances finally muttered. "Just…wow."

"I know."

"How did you find him?"

"I googled him and he came right up. He's this big shot real estate developer in San Francisco."

Frances sucked in a breath. "You don't think he'd want to buy the house, do you?"

"No way. He hates Christmas Bay, remember?" Still, Stella couldn't shake the fact that he'd seemed to perk up when she said the property was for sale. He'd asked several specific questions, the real estate kind, until her guard had shot up, leaving her uneasy.

"It's been a long time, honey. People change."

She shook her head. "Not Ian."

"Then why call him?"

"Because I thought if he gave the magazine a quick interview over the phone, it could help when the house goes on the market. You want a legitimate buyer, not some ghost hunters who will turn it into a tourist trap. You know people around here still talk about that silly story, and he's the only one who can put it to rest."

Frances looked skeptical. "But would he want to?"

"I'd hope so after what he put you through while he was here. Including making up that story in the first place and spreading it around. It's been years. I'd assumed he'd matured enough to at least feel a little bad about it."

Frances was quiet at that. She'd always defended Ian when he'd been defiant. He'd had this innate charm that seemed to sway most of the adults around him, but Stella had been able to see right through him. Maybe because she'd come from a similar background. Abuse, neglect. Nobody was going to pull the wool over her eyes, not even a boy as cute as Ian.

Suddenly looking wistful, maybe even a little regretful, Frances gazed out the window. The mist was beginning to burn off, and the sun was trying its best to poke through the steely clouds overhead. Even in the winter, Frances's yard was beautiful. Emerald green, and surrounded by golden Scotch broom that stretched all the way to the edge of the cliffs of Cape Longing. As a girl, Stella thought it looked like something out of *Wuthering Heights*. As a woman, she understood how special the property really was. And how valuable.

She truly hadn't believed Ian would be interested in the house, or she wouldn't have called him. It wasn't the kind of real estate he seemed to be making so much money on in the city, at least according to the internet. He and his business partner bought properties and built apartment buildings and housing developments on them, and the Cape Longing land was smaller than what they were probably used to. But after talking to him, even for just those few painful minutes, Stella knew he was more calculating than she'd given him credit for. If he smelled a good deal, even if it was in Christmas Bay, he might just follow his nose. Which was the *last* thing Frances needed.

"So, what did he say?" her foster mother asked. "Will he do the interview?"

"He wouldn't say. I never should've called him. I could just kick myself."

"At least you got to talk to him again."

Stella bit her tongue. *Yeah, at least.*

"Did he say how he was?" Frances asked hopefully. She was so sweet. And it made Stella indignant for her all over again. She'd loved and cared for Ian like he was her own, seeing something special in him, even under all the surliness and anger. She'd told him that often, but it didn't matter. He'd made his time with her miserable, and had ended up running away. He'd disappeared for days, worrying Frances sick, and ultimately breaking her heart when he was sent to live with a great-aunt instead, who also lived in Christmas Bay.

Stella had a hunch it was *because* of the love Frances had shown him, not in spite of it. If Ian sensed anyone getting close, he ran. He was a runner. She'd be willing to bet he'd run all these years, and had ended up in San Francisco, still the same old Ian. Just older. And maybe a little more jaded, if that was possible.

Stella liked to think that despite their similar background, one that had helped her understand him better than most people might, she'd turned out softer, more approachable. And she credited Frances for that. Maybe if Ian had stayed put, he might've had his rough edges smoothed out some, too.

She smiled at her foster mother, determined not to say what she was thinking. Determined to show some grace, at least for the time being. "We didn't get that far," she said. "I guess he had a meeting or something."

Frances nodded. "So, he's done well for himself?"

If his website was any indication, he was doing more than well.

"He seems to be."

"I wish things had turned out differently," Frances said. "I wish I could've reached him."

"It wasn't because you didn't try, Frances. We all did."

"But maybe if we'd tried harder..."

Frowning, Stella leaned forward and put a hand over Frances's. Her foster mother smelled good this morning. Like perfume and sugar cookies. She was in her early sixties, and was a beautiful, vital woman. Nobody would ever guess that she struggled with her memory as much as she did. So much so that her three foster daughters had moved back home to help her navigate this next chapter of her life.

In the corner of the sunroom, one of the house's two Christmas trees glittered. The decorations were ocean themed, of course. The blue lights glowed through the room like a lighthouse beacon. Christmas cards from previous foster children, now long grown, were strung around one of the double-paned windows. The old Victorian came alive over the holidays, and its warmth and coziness was one of the reasons Stella loved it so much. She knew it would be heartbreaking to sell it. Frances was right to want a family living here. Somehow, it softened the blow.

"You were the best thing to happen to us," Stella said quietly. "I'm just sorry he couldn't see that."

Frances smiled, but it looked like she was far away. Lost in her memories.

Stella scratched Beauregard behind his ears, before leaning back again with a sigh. Lost in some of hers.

Ian shifted the Porsche into second. This was the first time he'd driven it in the mountains, and not surprisingly, it hugged the hairpin turns like a dream. If he was in the mood, he'd be driving faster. After all, why own a German-engineered sports car if you weren't going to break the speed limit every now and then? But he wasn't in the mood. And getting to Christmas Bay any faster wasn't exactly tempting.

Gritting his teeth, he glanced out the window to the ocean on his left. Then at the GPS to his right. He'd be there in less than half an hour. Plenty of time to wonder about this decision. Yeah, the Cape Longing property might be the deal of a lifetime—*if* he could convince Frances to sell to him—but was it worth stepping foot back inside the little town he'd left so long ago? He wasn't so sure.

Which brought him back to Frances again. And to

Stella. Ian could smooth-talk anyone. Anyone having second thoughts, or experiencing cold feet, was putty in his hands after about five minutes. Less, over drinks. But true to form, Stella had been immune to everything he'd thrown at her over the phone. The conversation had turned stilted in *less* than five minutes, which he wasn't used to.

Thinking about it now, he bristled. She'd always been different than the rest of the kids he'd known in the system. Foster kids were usually wise, but she was wiser. They were tough, but she was tougher. They had walls, but Stella had barricades. He'd never been able to scale them, and then he'd just stopped trying. He didn't need anyone, anyway. Not Frances O'Hara, not Kyla or Marley, and sure as hell not Stella. So, he'd done anything and everything in his power to test them. He'd stolen, lied, smoked, drank. You name it, he'd done it. And for the cherry on the crapcake, he'd come up with that dumbass story about the ghost, knowing what a headache it would be for Frances. Knowing how it would get around and eventually stick in a town that was known for every kind of story sticking. Especially the bad kind.

But now, he had a chance to rectify it. That's what Stella had said. *Rectify.* Like he owed them something by talking to *Coastal Monthly* for their fluffy Christmas piece. *It's not like it matters*, he'd said evenly. *These days, a story like that only helps sell houses.*

And that's when she'd told him that Frances wanted

a family living there. Someone who would love it as much as she did.

When he'd hung up, he'd gotten an idea. Why *not* do the interview?

He'd tracked down the lady writing the article, and she'd practically begged him to come up to Christmas Bay so she could take pictures. And if he got a good look at the property in person, through the eyes of a real estate developer, well, then… What could it hurt? Other than shocking the hell out of Stella, who'd asked him to talk to the magazine but definitely would *not* expect him to do it in person. No way would she have wanted to open up that can of worms. She'd suspect a deeper motivation, and she'd be right.

In the beginning, money had been the driving force. Of course it had. But as he made his way up Highway 101, his Porsche winding along the cliffs overlooking the ocean, he had to admit there was another reason he was doing this. For once, it had nothing to do with money and everything to do with wanting to see Stella again. Just so she could see what he'd become. Just so he could flaunt it in her pretty face.

He downshifted again and glanced over at the water. It sparkled nearly as far as the eye could see. It was deep blue today, turquoise where the waves met the beach. The evergreens only added to the incredible palate of colors, standing tall and noble against the bluebird sky.

It had been so long since Ian had been up this way that he'd almost forgotten how beautiful it was. Easy, because the Bay Area was beautiful, too. But in a different way. There were so many people down there that sometimes it was hard to look past all the buildings and cars to see the nature beyond. On the Oregon Coast, the people were sparse. So sparse that it wasn't unusual to go to the beach and not see anyone at all. The weather had something to do with that—it was usually cold. But the scenery? The scenery was some of the most spectacular in the world, and Ian had been to a lot of places.

Swallowing hard, he passed a sign on his right. Christmas Bay, Ten Miles. Ten miles, and he'd be back in the town where he'd been the most miserable, the loneliest and most confused of his entire life. But also, where he'd caught a glimpse of what love could look like if he'd only let it in. But he hadn't let it in. In the end, he hadn't known how. And he'd been too pissed at the world to try, anyway.

There was absolutely no other reason, other than maybe a little spite, that he wanted to come back here again. No reason at all.

That's what he kept telling himself as the trees opened up, and Christmas Bay finally came into view.

Stella opened up the front door to see a woman in trendy glasses standing on the stoop. She looked the part of a journalist. Her hair was in a messy bun, and she had a camera bag slung over one shoulder. It was a beautiful day, perfect for pictures, but it was cold, and she was dressed appropriately for a December day on the Oregon Coast—rain boots and a thick cardigan.

When she saw Stella, she smiled wide. But her gaze immediately settled on the entryway behind her. It was obvious she couldn't wait to get a look inside.

"Hi, there," she said, holding out a hand. "Gwen Todd. And you must be Stella?"

Stella shook it. "I'm so glad the weather cooperated."

"Oh, I know. I thought it was going to pour. We got lucky."

"Please come in," Stella said. "Frances has some coffee brewing."

Gwen stepped past her and into the foyer. Before Stella could turn around, she heard the other woman gasp. She couldn't blame her. The house was incredible. Three stories of stunning Victorian charm. Gleaming hardwood floors, antique lamps that cast a warm, yellow glow throughout. A winding staircase that you immediately wanted to climb, just to see what treasures waited at the top. A widow's walk on the third floor that looked out over the cliffs, where Ian said he'd seen a ghost all those years ago. A coastal cliché that the entire town had latched onto, but that her family would finally shake free of today. At least, Stella hoped they would. It was just an article—it wasn't going to go viral or anything. But for the locals, for someone most likely to buy this house and live happily in it, it would be a start.

Gwen Todd ran her hand along the staircase's glossy banister. "Oh, it's just lovely. I've always wanted to see inside."

Stella had heard that more times than she could count. From certain places in town, you could see the house, perched high above Cape Longing, its distinctive yellow paint peeking like the sun through the gaps in the trees. It had been built when Christmas Bay was just a tiny logging settlement, and Frances's grandparents had had to get their supplies by boat, because the mountain roads were impassible by wagon in the winter and spring. As the town had grown, the house had become a fixture, near and far. It even had its own display in the local maritime museum—the fuzzy, black-and-white pictures taking people back to a time when the West was still fairly wild.

And Gwen Todd was clearly a fan. Shaking her head, she looked around, enthralled.

Stella smiled. She understood how Gwen felt, because that was exactly how she'd felt as a girl, walking through the doors of this place for the first time. In absolute wonder and awe. For a kid who'd gone from surviving on ramen noodles in a broken-down trailer on the outskirts of town, to this? It had been almost too good to be true. For the first six months of her new life with Frances, Stella had expected someone to come and take her away at any moment. Or worse, for her mother to get her back. She'd had nightmares about being deposited back into that cruelty and filth. Into that never-ending cycle of neglect and abuse. It wasn't until after the first full year that she'd begun to trust her good fortune. That she'd been able to start opening her heart again. Cautiously, and just a little at a time.

Now, standing here, those days seemed so far away, they were just as fuzzy as the pictures in the museum down the road. But other times, they were clear as a bell, and those were the days that tended to hit her the hardest. When the pain and memories were too sharp to take a full breath. Thank God for Frances. Otherwise, there was no telling where she would've ended up. Or *how* she would've ended up. She hadn't spoken to her biological parents in years. She simply had nothing to say to them.

Gwen looked at her watch, just as Frances walked in holding out a reindeer mug full of steaming coffee. This time of year, Frances served all her drinks in Christmas mugs. She was proud of her collection.

"Oh, thanks so much," Gwen said. "This will help wake me up before Mr. Steele gets here."

Stella froze. Frances froze, too.

"I'm sorry," Stella managed. "What?"

"Mr. Steele. He's supposed to be here at eleven, but I think he might be running late…"

Stella stared at Frances, who sank down in a chair by the staircase. She looked pale.

"Oh…" Gwen set her coffee cup down. "Oh, no. I thought I mentioned that he'd be coming?"

"I don't think so," Stella said. There was no way she'd mentioned that. Stella would've remembered.

"There were so many calls back and forth, I must've totally spaced it. I'm so sorry. Will it be a problem?"

Gwen looked genuinely concerned, but if she'd known exactly how Ian had left things all those years ago, Stella knew she'd be downright horrified. He hadn't stepped foot inside this house since he'd left with his social worker at sixteen. Frances had been crying. She'd stood at the window watching them pull out of the driveway with tears streaming down her face. She'd felt like she'd failed him. Which was ridiculous, but that's how she'd felt, which made Stella furious with him all over again.

She forced a smile to ease Gwen's mind. And maybe her own, too. There was always the chance he'd show up and apologize to Frances for how he'd treated her back then. Or that he'd acknowledge that what he'd said at that coffee date years ago had been horribly untrue—suggesting their sweet and loving foster mother had only taken them in for the money. A disgusting comment that had brought up every single insecurity that Stella had ever had about finding a genuine home. But she doubted he'd do either of those things. She also doubted that he was coming back to Christmas Bay simply to do this interview and help Frances sell her house. No way. He had other motives in mind. Probably like getting a good look at her property, since, like an idiot, Stella had practically waved it in his face.

"It's okay," she said. "We just haven't seen him in a long time. He was one of Frances's foster kids, and he left…suddenly."

Gwen frowned, glancing at Frances, and then back at Stella again. "Are you sure? I feel terrible about this. I wouldn't want it to be awkward for you."

Too late.

Frances shook her head. "No, honey. Don't worry. He's come all this way to do the interview, so that says a lot. Maybe this is a blessing in disguise."

As if on cue, there was the roar of a car coming up the drive. All three of them moved over to the bay window and looked out, like they were waiting for Santa Claus or something. Stella crossed her arms over her chest, annoyed by her own curiosity. She didn't care that she'd be seeing Ian again. She couldn't stand him and his giant ego. And she managed to believe that. Mostly.

Outside, a beautiful silver sports car pulled into view, mud from the long dirt driveway spattered on its glossy paint job. Stella's heart beat heavily inside her chest as she saw the silhouette of a man through the tinted windows. Short black hair, straight nose and strong jaw. Sunglasses that concealed eyes that she remembered all too well. Blue, like Caribbean water. But not nearly as warm.

Letting out a low breath, she watched as the door opened, and he stepped out. Tall, broad shouldered and dressed impeccably in a crisp, white-collared shirt and khaki slacks. Like the car, the clothes looked expensive. Tailored to his lean body in a way that she'd really only seen in magazines. So, this was how Ian had turned out. Probably with an even bigger ego than she'd remembered.

Frances looked over at her. "I can't believe how handsome he is. He looks so different."

There were differences. But there were also similarities, and those were what made Stella's chest tighten as she watched him swipe his dark sunglasses off and walk toward the front door with that same old confidence. That same old arrogance that had driven her bananas as a kid. That had driven them *all* bananas.

But there was no doubt he'd grown into that confidence. As a woman, she could imagine feeling safe and secure in his presence. And at that, she recoiled. Nothing about Ian Steele should make her feel safe. He was a piranha, only here for a meal. She'd bet her life on it.

Beside them, Gwen cleared her throat and touched her hair. Probably taken with his looks—something that made Stella want to snap her fingers in front of her face. *Snap out of it, Gwen!*

Instead, she walked over to the front door and opened it with her features perfectly schooled.

He stood with his hands in his pockets, gazing down at her like she was some acquaintance he was meeting for lunch. Instead of a girl he'd shared a home with, a family with, for two tumultuous years.

He smiled, and his straight white teeth flashed against his tanned skin. Two long dimples cut into each cheek. *Good God, he's grown into a good-looking man.* The kind of man who stopped traffic. Or at least a heart or two.

Stella stood there, stoic. Reminding herself that it didn't matter how he looked. It only mattered that he gave this interview and went on his merry way again. Got back in his sports car and got the heck out of Christmas Bay.

"Stella," he said, that Caribbean gaze sweeping her entire body. He didn't bother trying to hide it. "It's been a long time."

She stiffened. If he was trying to unnerve her, it wasn't going to work. He might be trying to brush those two years underneath the rug, but she sure wasn't going to. He'd made their lives miserable, and had left a lasting scar on Frances's heart. Something she refused to minimize or forgive. And that slippery smile said he wasn't the least bit sorry about what he'd said over that fateful coffee date. Whether he'd meant it or not, he'd definitely wanted to wound her, probably since she'd stayed and found happiness in

Christmas Bay, and he hadn't. No, he wasn't sorry. Not by a longshot.

"Ian," she said. "Exactly the same, I see."

His smile only widened at that. "Now, how can you say that? It's been years."

"Oh, I can tell." She glanced over her shoulder into the living room. Frances and Gwen were talking in low tones, obviously waiting for her to bring him inside. She looked back at him and narrowed her eyes. "I know exactly why you're here."

"I don't know what you're talking about."

"Cut the crap, Ian. Frances wouldn't sell to you if you were the last man on earth."

Rubbing the back of his neck, he seemed to contemplate that. "Oh, you mean because the house is coming up on the market, and I'm a real estate developer, you just assumed I'm here to schmooze…"

"I *know* you're here to schmooze," she whisper-yelled. "But it's not going to work. You're not going to just waltz in here after all this time and get what you want. Life doesn't work that way."

"Oh, I beg to differ. It does, in fact, work that way." He leaned back in his expensive Italian loafers and looked down his nose at her. "Are you going to invite me in, or are we going to stand here and argue all day? I mean, don't get me wrong, the sexual tension is nice, but there's a time and place for it."

She felt the blood rush to her cheeks. "Give me a break."

He smiled again, his eyes twinkling. She wanted to murder him. But that wouldn't be good for the sale of the house, either, so she stepped stiffly aside as he walked past, trying not to breathe in his subtle, musky cologne that smelled like money.

When Frances saw him, she took a noticeable breath. Then she stepped forward and pulled him into a hug. He was so tall, she had to stand on her tiptoes to do it. But he bent down obligingly, even though Stella could tell his body was unyielding. Ian had always had trouble with giving and receiving affection.

Stella couldn't bring herself to feel sorry for him. He'd had plenty of opportunities to be loved. Frances had tried, but he'd only pushed her away. It was what it was.

Still, she couldn't help but notice how his jaw was clenched, the muscles bunching and relaxing methodically. How his gaze was fixed on the wall behind Frances, stony and cold. Like he just wanted to retreat. And before she could help it, there was a flutter of compassion for him, after all. Because she could remember feeling the same way a long time ago.

After a second, he pulled away and looked down at her with a careful smile on his face. Not the almost-playful one he'd given Stella a minute before. This one was more structured. Like he'd been practicing it awhile. Like fifteen years, maybe.

"Hi, Frances," he said. "It's good to see you."

Stella could see that she was having a hard time with a reply. Her eyes were definitely misty. Poor Frances. She'd just wanted the kids who'd passed through her doors to leave happy. She'd wanted to give them a home, whether it was for a few months, or the rest of their childhoods. The fact that she hadn't been able to give Ian any of those things still bothered her. Probably because, despite that carefully crafted smile, his pain was clearly visible. It had been brought right to the surface by this visit. Stella had to wonder if he'd been prepared for that when he'd hatched this asinine plan.

"Ian," Frances said. "You grew up."

"Probably all those vitamins you made me take."

"Well, they worked. Just look at you."

Gwen stepped forward and fluttered her lashes. She actually fluttered her lashes. Stella wanted to groan.

"Oh, I'm sorry," Frances said. "Gwen, this is Ian Steele. Ian, this is Gwen Todd, from *Coastal Monthly.*"

Ian took her hand, appearing just short of kissing it. Gwen didn't seem to mind. In fact, her cheeks flushed pink.

"Gwen, it's a pleasure."

"Thank you so much for making the drive up," she said. "I know it's a long one, but I'm so glad you did."

Stella eyed him, waiting for him to admit to wanting to take a look at the house, even in passing. Otherwise, why not do the interview over the phone?

But he didn't. He just smiled down at Gwen inno-cently. *Who me? I just want to help with the article, that's all...*

Frances took all this in with interest. If she was worried about Ian's true intentions, she didn't let on. She just seemed happy to see him again. Which, in Stella's opinion, he didn't deserve. But that was Frances for you. Kind to the core.

Clapping her hands together, Gwen smiled. "Are we ready? I thought maybe we could start with some pictures of the upstairs, Frances. Maybe the widow's walk?"

"Sounds good to me."

"Me, too," Ian said.

Stella stepped forward, narrowly missing Ian's toe. All of a sudden, Frances's spacious living room seemed as big as a postage stamp. She stepped back again, putting some distance between them, but not before catching his smirk. Of course he was enjoy-ing this. Of course he was.

"The widow's walk is where Ian said he saw the ghost," Stella said tightly. "Are you sure you want to put that in the article, Frances? Maybe we shouldn't focus on that part?"

Frances frowned. "That's true…"

"Well, that's no problem," Gwen said, fishing her camera out of the bag. "We'll just start with a few by the Christmas tree, and then we can go outside to the garden. The sun is coming out. The light should be perfect."

Stella smiled, relieved. As long as things went smoothly, this article might actually end up painting the house in the light it deserved, which was what she'd hoped for in the beginning. And maybe she was just being paranoid as far as Ian was concerned. Maybe after he got a look at the place, he'd dismiss it like he probably dismissed so many other things in his life. After all, this was Christmas Bay, and what she'd told Frances was true. He hated Christmas Bay.

He stepped up to the bay window and looked out toward the ocean. The muscles in his jaw were bunching again, his blue eyes narrowing in the sunlight.

"My God, I'd almost forgotten that view," he said under his breath. Almost too softly for anyone else to hear.

But Stella heard. And even though it had been years since she'd seen Ian Steele, or that look in his eyes, she recognized it immediately.

This was something he wanted. And he intended to get it.

Chapter Two

Ian walked behind Stella, having trouble keeping his eyes off her amazing rear end. She'd been slightly overweight as a kid, always refusing to get into a swimsuit at the city pool. She'd worn a T-shirt and shorts instead, which he'd thought was dumb. She'd looked just fine, but the girls he knew had a way of obsessing over things like that. If it wasn't their weight, it was their skin. Or their hair. Or a myriad of other things. Even the prettiest ones, who had absolutely nothing to worry about, worried, anyway. Stella had been that way.

But he could see those days were long gone. She was no longer the girl in the oversize clothes. She was a confident, stunningly beautiful woman, who was looking over her shoulder at him like she wanted to stick a knife between his ribs.

"Be careful," she said. "The railing is wobbly."

They were climbing the stairs to the widow's walk, after all. Frances had changed her mind, and thought it would be a fitting end to the article to have a picture of Ian standing there, looking out over the ocean. A grown man, coming back to the place where he'd spent so much time as a boy. A place that, as a confused, overwhelmed kid, he'd once said was haunted, but that he now realized was only a sweet old house that didn't deserve a dark reputation. The whole thing was a little too cute for his taste, but that's what people around here liked. Stella was absolutely right, thinking this article would help sell the house. That is, if he didn't get his hands on it first.

He smiled up at her, running his hand along the railing. "I remember."

She didn't smile back. Just turned around and kept climbing, her lovely backside only inches from his face. Good Lord, he really was a jackass. But he couldn't help it. She had a gorgeous body, and his gaze was drawn to it like it was magnetized. It wasn't like he wasn't used to gorgeous bodies, either. The women he usually dated were high maintenance, and keeping themselves up was part of their lifestyle. But Stella's body was soft, curvaceous. Something he could imagine running his hands over, exploring, undressing. Her skin would probably be just as velvety as her voice, and at the thought, his throat felt uncomfortably tight.

Taking the last few steps up the narrow, winding staircase, he stepped out behind her on the widow's walk. Frances and Gwen were already standing near the iron railing, looking out over the ocean. He stared at it, too, and for a few seconds, all thoughts of Stella's body were forgotten in favor of the house's property value.

He fished his sunglasses out of his front pocket and put them on. The yard below was spacious and pretty. A peeling white picket fence that was covered in climbing vines and rosebushes enveloped it like a hug. In the summer, the whole space was alive with colorful, fragrant blooms that made the garden look like something out of a fairy tale. In the winter, it was more subdued, but still a beautiful, luscious green.

Beyond the yard was the ever-present Scotch broom that butted right up to the edge of the cliffs that dropped into the sea. Cape Longing was one of the most dramatic stretches along the Oregon Coast, and finding land here that was prime for development was rare. Ian's wheels were turning so fast, he could barely think straight. *Condos.* He could picture a small row of expensive condos or town houses. Simple, midcentury modern style, with lots of glass and metal. Balconies that overlooked the sea. Perfect for reading, or having a glass of wine, or entertaining in the evenings. Bachelor pads, or a couple's paradise... They could go in any direction, appeal to anyone. And with a setting like this, he could sell them for more than he'd even dreamed.

He looked up to see Frances smiling over at him.

"I hope you have some good memories of being up here," she said. "I know this used to be your favorite part of the house."

He smiled back, determined not to let that get to him. Determined not to tumble back into the past, to those lonely nights when he'd sat up here, looking out at the ocean reflecting the full moon above. Feeling scared and alone, and then ashamed for feeling so scared and alone. He guessed that's where that stupid ghost story of his had come from. Underneath everything, it had been a cry for help, a bid for attention. And now he was going to debunk it very publicly, in this article. If he owed Frances anything, that was it. And then they'd be even as far as he was concerned. She wasn't going to look at him with those doe eyes, and make him feel guilty for seeing a good business opportunity here. She just wasn't.

"I wasn't always easy to live with," he said, "but I do have some good memories of this place."

He was in the beginning stages of buttering her up, but maybe that was a bridge too far. It's not that it wasn't true—he did have good memories. Not that he'd ever admitted that...until now. But he could feel Stella watching him from a few feet away, her gaze like a laser beam boring into his head.

"Oh, really?" she muttered.

He turned to her. She knew exactly what he was thinking. He didn't know how, but she did. Not that it mattered. Frances was the only one who mattered here. It wasn't Stella who would be choosing a buyer, it was Frances.

"Really," he said.

"I'm glad to hear that," Frances said. "So glad."

Gwen was fiddling with her camera, looking like she was trying to get the lighting right. "So, this was where you said you saw the ghost?" she asked, holding the camera up and peering through the lens.

"This was the spot," he said. "Only, you know by now I didn't really see anything."

Gwen lowered the camera again. "So, why did you do it? Why did you make up that story?"

"Because I had a problem with the truth back then. Troubled kid, going off the rails—you know the drill."

Gwen nodded. Behind her, Frances frowned, her expression sad.

Back then, Ian hadn't believed her when she'd said she cared about him. He hadn't believed anyone when they'd told him anything. His mother had lied over and over and over again. About her relationships, about Ian's future with her. About everything. So, he'd learned to lie, too. And he'd learned to use lies to get exactly what he wanted.

Stella kept watching him. Maybe waiting for him

to apologize. What the hell—he needed to stay on Frances's good side, anyway.

He let his gaze settle on the older woman with the kind eyes. He'd resented her so much back then. She'd been just another adult forcing him into a mold that he'd never wanted or asked for. *Troubled kid, going off the rails*... But he could never quite lump her into the same category as his parents and everyone else who'd let him down over the years. She was different then. She was different now.

"I'm sorry, Frances," he said. He had been bitter about his time in foster care, and she'd been a convenient target. She'd remained one for a long time, even after he'd left Christmas Bay. But she hadn't deserved his behavior. Today, he found he could say the words, but he still couldn't forgive her in his heart. Even though that was ridiculous, of course—none of it had been her fault. But he still couldn't get past her role in all of it. He'd been taken away from the only home he'd ever known and placed with a complete stranger, and the anger had nearly eaten him alive.

But he could at least say the words. And the words were all he needed right now.

She smiled, clearly moved. *Goal achieved*.

"Honey, you have nothing to be sorry for. It's all behind us now."

It wasn't behind them. Not by a long shot, since he was acutely aware that he was still lying for his own benefit. In this case, that benefit was her house. But he'd said he was sorry, and she seemed to accept it, and in that way, they could move forward. He could pile on the charm, convince her to sell, make a ton of money and leave Christmas Bay in his rearview mirror. This time for good.

"Frances," Gwen said, "why don't you move over to the railing next to Ian, and I can get a picture of you both."

"Oh, that's a good idea. Stella, why don't you get in here with us?"

Stella shook her head. "No, that's okay. This one can be just you two."

"Are you sure?"

"Positive."

Ian watched her as Frances walked over, leaning into his side for the picture. She watched him back, her blue eyes chilly. Her long dark hair moved in the ocean breeze. It was wild around her face, wavy, but not quite curly. Her skin was pale, delicate. Almost translucent, and there was a spattering of freckles across her nose. She was so pretty that he could almost forget how he'd never been able to stand her.

But even as he thought it, even as Gwen told them to smile and say cheese, he couldn't believe that same old line he'd always repeated to himself. He hated Frances. He hated Stella. He hated Marley and Kyla, and all the other foster kids who'd come in and out of the house during his time there. But the truth, which Ian still had trouble with, was more complicated than that. More layered. He hadn't really hated them. The truth was, he'd *wanted* to hate them, and there was a difference.

"Perfect," Gwen said, lowering the camera again. "I think that's about it. I've got everything I need. I'll call you if the gaps need filling in, but I think this is going to be a great Christmas article."

Frances touched Gwen's elbow. "Let me walk you out."

And just like that, Ian found himself alone with Stella. Just the two of them, facing each other on the widow's walk, the salty breeze blowing through their hair. He caught her scent, something clean, flowery. Something that made his groin tighten.

"We might as well not beat around the bush," he said evenly. "I'm going to be honest with you."

"Well, that's a first."

"I'm interested in this property, you're right. I think it's a great development opportunity."

Her lovely eyes flashed. "I knew it. I knew that's why you came."

"I came because I owed it to Frances. And I was curious about the house, too."

"You're so full of it, Ian. You were *only* curious about the house."

She was going to think what she was going to think. There was nothing he could do about it, and he didn't care, anyway.

He leaned casually against the railing and smiled

down at her. Something he remembered had always driven her crazy. "Now that I've seen it," he said, "I'm going to talk to Frances about making an offer."

"Forget it. She'll never sell to you."

"Says who?"

"Says me."

"Last I checked, you don't own it."

She glared up at him. "No, but she'll listen to me. She'll listen to Marley and Kyla. And all we'll have to do is remind her that she wants a family here."

"She may have some romantic notion of selling to a family, but in reality, money talks. And I think she'll sell for the right price."

"You're insufferable," she bit out. She was furious now. Her cheeks were pink, her full lips pursed. Before he could help it, he wondered what she'd be like in bed. All that passion and energy directed right at him. But that wasn't a fantasy that had a chance of coming true anytime soon. By the looks of it, she'd rather run him over with her car first.

"Don't assume Frances would just sell to the highest bidder," she continued. "She doesn't need the money. Despite what you've always thought."

She was obviously talking about that idiotic comment he'd made about Frances's motives that night at the coffee shop in Portland. Something he'd said out of bitterness. It had been a rotten thing to say, not to mention categorically untrue. Stella hadn't given him a chance to take it back, though. She'd gotten up and slammed out before he could utter another word. Fast-forward almost ten years, and now here they were.

"I didn't mean that," he said huskily. "What I said back then."

She crossed her arms over her chest.

"And I know she doesn't need the money *now*," he continued. "But what about later? On the phone, you said she's got Alzheimer's. That's why she can't handle the house anymore. Retirement homes are expensive. Care facilities are even more expensive. This would give her a nest egg for her future. She's smart—she's got to know she'll need one."

Stella gaped at him. "Oh, you are disgusting. You're even lower than I thought you'd be when you showed up here, and believe me, that's pretty low."

"How is it low? The way I see it, I'd be helping her out."

"You *would* see it that way." She shook her head, her dark hair blowing in front of her face. She tucked it behind her ears and took a deep breath. "She wants a family here, and that's the only thing that's going to sway her. Believe me, you don't stand a chance."

He put his hands in his pockets. "Hmm."

"What?"

"I'm just saying, if she wants a family living here, I might fit the bill there, too."

She laughed. "What? Come on."

"I don't have a family. Yet. But eventually I might,

and it'd be great to have the house checked off the list." She was right. He *was* low.

Stella watched him suspiciously. "You just said this place is a great development opportunity. You expect me to believe you'd actually live here?"

"I might. For a while."

"Baloney. You're just saying that to get what you want."

"Believe me, don't believe me. Doesn't matter to me, Stella. What matters to me is what Frances believes. And by the way, this whole archrival thing we've got going on? It's only making me want the house more."

"Oh, really."

"Really."

"You'd buy a house out of spite?"

"No, I'd buy a house to make money. I'd sell it out of spite."

She glared up at him. She was fuming. But if she thought she was going to stand in his way, she was wrong. Nobody stood in his way. At least not people who didn't want to get bulldozed.

After a second, she looked away. She stared out at the ocean that was sparkling underneath the midday sun. He couldn't be sure, but he thought her chin might be trembling a little. And if it was, that would be a surprise. A crack in her otherwise impenetrable armor.

"Hey," he said.

She didn't look at him. Just continued staring at the water.

He took a breath, not sure what to say. Taken off guard by her sudden show of emotion. Ian could take a lot of things, and did on a daily basis. But the sight of a woman crying had always unnerved him. Talk about an Achilles heel. He remembered walking in on Stella crying once when they were kids. She'd been trying to be quiet, so as not to call attention to herself. She'd looked up at him, her cheeks wet with tears, and the expression on her face had nearly broken his heart. He remembered very clearly wanting to cross the room to hug her, to comfort her. To take some of her pain away, just a little.

"You can tell me to go to hell," he said now. "But I'll give you some advice, Stella. Sometimes there's such a thing as caring too much."

At that she looked back at him. And he'd been right. There were tears in her eyes. He had to stop himself before he reached for her, because really, she was a stranger to him. He didn't know her anymore, and he didn't care to know her. He was only here for a business deal.

"She's eventually going to forget all the memories she has of this place," she said. "The only thing that comforts her is the thought of someone making new memories here. For me, as far as Frances is concerned, there is no such thing as caring too much."

He grit his teeth. *There's no such thing…* He wondered how it was that they'd ended up so differently. Her caring too much, and him not caring at all. They were two stars at the opposite ends of the universe. And she still shone just as brightly as she had when she was fourteen. Maybe he was jealous of that. Deep down. Maybe he wanted to love just as fiercely as Stella Clarke did.

She lifted her chin. "So, yes, Ian. You can take your money, and your offer, and you can go to hell."

And she walked out.

"Here's your room key, sir." The woman smiled up at him, wrinkles exploding from the corners of her brown eyes. Her Christmas tree earrings sparkled, coming in a close second to her sweater. She looked like Mrs. Claus.

"Thank you," he said.

"There's a vending machine right down the breezeway, and if you want to rent a movie, we have a pretty good selection of DVDs, but the front desk closes at nine."

He took the key card and tucked it in his back pocket, preoccupied with the events of that afternoon. Frances owned a candy shop on Main Street, and she and Stella had gone back to work right after their meeting with Gwen. That had left him zero time to approach her about the house, so he'd made the incredibly annoying decision to stay in Christmas Bay overnight.

He'd called and asked if he could meet Frances for coffee before heading home tomorrow, and she'd seemed genuinely happy about that. He'd make his move then. Her defenses were already down because of this cheesy article. If he could frame the sale in a way that would tug on her heartstrings, it would be easier than he'd thought.

Pushing down the slightest feeling of guilt, he grabbed a razor, comb and toothbrush from a rack beside the counter and paid quickly, not wanting to encourage any more small talk with the Jingle Bell Inn front desk lady. He'd already had to endure enough nosy questions—what brought him to town, where had he bought a car that fancy, etcetera, etcetera. All topped off with a story about someone who'd stayed here not long ago who drove a Ferrari. The kind Tom Selleck had in *Magnum P.I.* He'd smiled and nodded politely. But inside, he was dying. This was exactly the kind of interaction he never had to deal with in the city. In the city, people couldn't care less why you were staying overnight. They just took your credit card and told you where the best seafood places were.

Gathering his things, he told the lady to have a good evening and walked out the door. The sun was just beginning its fiery descent toward the ocean. The sky was a brilliant swirl of pinks and purples, and the salty breeze felt good on his skin. He breathed in the smell of the water, of the beach, letting the air saturate his lungs. Letting it bring him back, just a little, to the last time he was here.

He'd left his aunt Betty's and Christmas Bay the second he'd graduated from high school—right after he'd turned eighteen and was done with the foster system for good. His mother had made some weak overtures about him coming to live with her again, and letting her "help" him with college. He hadn't been able to tell her off fast enough. This, after an entire childhood of not caring whether he was coming or going, or that he'd basically served as a punching bag for her ever-revolving door of boyfriends.

He slid the key card into the lock, watching the light blink green, then opened the door and walked into the small room with his stomach in a knot. He really couldn't believe he was back here after all this time. He'd never planned on it. His mother had passed away a few years ago, and the only relative still living here was a great-aunt who was in a retirement home across town. He'd gone to live with her after he'd left Frances's house for good. She'd tried to make a connection with him, and had been the only one in his family who ever acted like they cared at all. But he'd kept her at an arm's length, anyway, protecting himself the best way he knew how. The thought of coming back to visit her had never crossed his mind. He'd left. And that meant leaving her, and everything else, behind, too.

Opening the sliding glass door, he stepped onto

the balcony with the beginnings of a headache throbbing at his temples. The guilt he'd felt earlier had settled in his gut like a small stone. If he had any chance of convincing Frances to sell to him, he needed to bury that guilt, along with any strange pull he was feeling toward Stella. These people were simply part of his past. They had no place in his future. And if they registered in his present at all, it was only because they were a means to an end.

It wasn't in Ian's nature to let fruit like this slip through his fingers once he realized how ripe it was for the picking. And no matter what kind of bleeding-heart reasons Frances had for wanting to sell her house to a family, he knew he'd been absolutely right about her needing the most money she could get out of it. What kind of local family would be able to come up with the cash to outbid him? What he was doing would only end up helping her, not hurting her.

Sinking down in one of the plastic deck chairs, he watched the waves pound the beach. In the distance, a woman was being dragged along by her golden retriever, the dog barking joyously at the water. Up ahead, two boys in hoodies were playing football in the sand. Other than that, the beach was empty. So unlike San Francisco, where the amount of people on a sunny winter day could make you feel like you couldn't catch your breath. Which, normally, he didn't mind. The hustle was what he liked about California. The opportunities, the possibilities. But the deep breathing you could do up here was undeniable.

He leaned back in the chair and pulled out his phone to do some quick calculations. How much the house might be worth on the market, how much the land alone might be worth and what kind of builders might be interested. Ian had instantly seen a few luxury condos perched on that cliff in his mind's eye. But honestly, it would be a great place for a high end spa, too. Maybe even a small, quaint hotel… He'd been worried the house would be on the National Register of Historic Places, but miraculously, it wasn't. Probably because it had always been a private residence and nobody famous had stayed there. Or maybe Frances's family had never gotten around to listing it. He knew there was an in-depth nomination process. Either way, his initial worry that he'd run into red tape was null and void.

Looking out over the water, he rubbed his chin. The golden retriever was in the surf now, its owner standing with her hands on her hips, looking resigned. She'd lost the battle. Despite his headache, Ian smiled. It was a Norman Rockwell kind of moment. But then again, Christmas Bay was a Norman Rockwell kind of town. Scratch that. It was for some people. For people like him, he remembered how dead-end and limiting it really was. Yeah, Frances would definitely be thanking him after this. Even if he did have to stretch the truth initially, she'd thank him in the end.

He'd bet on it.

"Frances, I'm not sure you realize who you're dealing with here, that's all."

Stella leaned against the counter next to the cash register, watching her foster mother go from window to window with a bottle of Windex and a wad of paper towels. She was just about done, and the glass was crystal clear. It wouldn't last, though. When you worked in a candy shop, you got used to fingerprints everywhere. Even some nose prints thrown in for good measure.

Frances didn't turn around. Just kept spraying and wiping, spraying and wiping. "I know you're worried, honey. But we're only going to have coffee. I'll just see what he has to say."

"I *know* what he's going to say."

"I keep telling you, people change."

"Yeah, sometimes they get worse."

"You still think he's selfish."

"Does the Pope wear a funny hat?"

Frances laughed. "Well. That would be a yes."

"I'm just saying, we spent an hour with the guy, and that was plenty. He's only here to make money. He doesn't care about the house."

Frances did turn around at that. "What kind of person would I be, what kind of foster mother, if I didn't at least hear him out? If I didn't give him a chance to prove himself?"

Stella sighed.

"You're just going to have to trust me on this one, Stella. I know my memory is going, but it's not gone yet, and I need to give him a chance."

Frowning, Stella chewed the inside of her cheek. Damn him. Frances was already being swayed by that big-city charm. By those blue eyes and that calculating smile. He probably knew exactly how Frances felt about him, and was going to use that to his fullest advantage. But at the end of the day, this was Frances's house, Frances's decision. All Stella could do was try to advise and be there for support.

"I do want you to come, though," Frances said, walking over and setting the Windex on the counter. "Would you do that for me?"

Stella's chest tightened. She hadn't been prepared to see him again so soon. Or maybe ever. The thought of looking up into that smug face made her want to chug a glass of wine.

She licked her lips, which suddenly felt dry. "What about the shop?"

"We'll close it. It's just for a little while."

Well, there goes that excuse.

She forced a smile. "Then of course I'll come."

"But you have to promise not to kill him."

"I can't promise that."

Frances reached out and took her hand, suddenly

looking serious. Almost desperate in a way, and Stella knew she was asking for reassurance. And comfort.

"I can't explain it," Frances said, "but I just want him to leave on good terms this time. Things with Ian have bothered me for years. This is a way to fix it, even if it's just to smooth it over. I need that. Can you understand?"

She could. She knew the sale of the house was the beginning of smoothing a lot of things over for Frances. She was settling her affairs, mending broken fences, looking back on mistakes she felt she'd made. And no matter how much Stella mistrusted Ian, she had to respect how Frances felt about him. Her foster children were her children. No matter how long they ended up staying with her. And having one of her children out there in the world, alone, unanchored, was too much for her to take, without at least having coffee with him and hearing him out, apparently.

Stella squeezed her hand. Frances had beautiful hands. Soft, and perfectly manicured, her nails usually painted some kind of fuchsia or cotton candy pink. Today, they were Christmas themed, green with little red polka dots.

"I can understand that, Frances," she said. "And I won't kill him. I promise."

Chapter Three

Ian sat in the sunroom of the old Victorian, with Stella sitting directly across from him. Frances had gone into the kitchen to get the coffee and pastries, insisting that "you kids sit and chat" for a minute.

So far there hadn't been any chatting. Just the chilly gaze of a woman who looked even more beautiful today than she had yesterday, if that was possible. She wore a gray Portland Trail Blazers hoodie and had her dark hair pulled into a high ponytail. Her face was freshly scrubbed, her cheeks pink and dewy. She still looked like she wanted to push him in front of a bus, though. Which was fine. Whatever.

He smiled at her and leaned back in the wicker chair. Everything in this room was wicker. Even the coffee table. It felt like he'd been teleported back to 1985.

"I wasn't expecting you to show up today," he said. "You seem like you'd rather be doing something else. Like getting a root canal, maybe."

Her lips twitched at that. But if he thought the teasing would get her to relax, he was sadly mistaken.

"That would be preferable, yes."

"Then why are you here?"

"Frances asked me to come, and I couldn't say no."

"Even though you wanted to."

"Exactly. But I promised I'd behave, so this is me behaving."

"Good to know. I'd hate to see you misbehaving."

A tubby black-and-white cat sauntered in with a hoarse meow, and blinked up at him through yellow eyes. Then it proceeded to wind itself around his ankles.

Ian stared down at it. He hated cats. He was allergic. In fact, he thought he could feel the beginnings of a tickle in his nose.

"Beauregard," Stella said. "No."

The cat looked over at her, unconcerned. Then he turned around and rammed his little head into Ian's shin.

"Beauregard." She leaned down and snapped her fingers at him, but he ignored her completely. Ian had to work not to laugh. He didn't like cats, but he did appreciate them. They did what the hell they wanted, when the hell they wanted to do it. If they came to you, it was because you had something to offer. If

they left, it was because something else was more appealing at that moment. As a human, he could relate.

He reached up and rubbed his nose. Definitely a tickle.

"Oh, I see you've met Beauregard," Frances said, appearing in the doorway with a tray. "Just nudge him with your foot if he's being a pest."

Ian nudged him, but the cat only seemed encouraged by the contact. He immediately came back for more.

"Oh, dear," Frances said, setting the tray down on the coffee table. "I think you've made a friend."

Ian looked down at him dubiously.

Sitting beside Stella, Frances handed over his coffee. "Black, like you said."

"Thank you."

"Honey," she said, handing Stella a cup. "Here you go."

"Thanks, Frances."

"That's homemade blackberry jam for the scones. Kyla and Marley made it last summer." She smiled over at Ian. "They came back to Christmas Bay, too. They're busy with their own families, but we see each other nearly every day, don't we, Stella?"

Stella took a sip of her coffee, eyeing him over the rim of the mug. A Christmas tree, draped in blue lights, twinkled next to her. The ocean outside the windows was gray and misty today. The perfect backdrop to the house on the cliff. It all felt like a movie set, and he was about to deliver his lines. The ones he'd rehearsed last night. The ones Frances wouldn't be able to resist.

He took a sip of his coffee, too, and burned his tongue. Wincing, he set it on the coffee table.

"Frances," he said evenly. "I want to talk to you about your house."

Clasping her hands in her lap, she waited. She'd obviously known this was coming. Stella sat beside her with a tight expression on her face. But whatever warning she'd given Frances, it obviously hadn't been enough to dissuade her from meeting with him today.

Sensing an opening, he leaned forward and put his elbows on his knees. "I'd like you to consider selling it to me."

She nodded slowly. "Is that the reason you came up here? To make an offer on the house?"

"I could've made an offer from San Francisco," he said, pushing down that annoying sliver of guilt that kept pricking at his subconscious. It was absolutely true. He could've made an offer from California, but he'd come up to do the interview, and he'd done it. He'd also come up for the house, but again, she didn't have to know that. Right now he needed to work the seller. He'd done it a thousand times before. Frances was no different.

"I wanted to do the interview for you. But when

I saw this place again…" He clasped his hands and looked around. "Well, I really couldn't resist."

"It's a beautiful house," Frances said. "And you have to know what it means to me."

"I do."

"I was raised here. And my parents and grandparents, too. And then all of you kids…"

He clenched his jaw. *You kids…* He still couldn't believe she thought of him as more than just a shithead teenager who'd slept here for a couple of years.

Pushing that down, he smiled. "I know. The emotional value far exceeds the monetary value. But I have to be honest, Frances. That's a lot, too."

"I don't care about the money."

He didn't believe that. Everyone cared about the money.

He licked his lips. Stella watched him steadily, saying *I told you so* with that cool gaze of hers.

Taking a page from the cat's playbook—who right that minute had his sizable girth spread out on Ian's foot—he ignored Stella and doubled down on Frances. If he wasn't careful, he'd lose control of the room, and he never lost control of the room.

"I know you don't," he said softly. Shaking his head. Milking the moment. "I know you want someone living here who will love it just like you do."

Her kind eyes, which had been slightly guarded a minute ago, warmed at that. He could hardly believe it was going to be this simple. But he went on, not wanting to lose any ground, and not trusting Stella to interrupt when he was just getting to the good stuff.

"I'm not married yet," he said. "But of course, I'd like to be someday." For such a whopping lie, it rolled off his tongue fairly easily. He just had to keep reminding himself that it could be true. Technically. Anything was possible.

"And I'd love this house just as much as you do, Frances," he finished. That part was downright true. He'd love the massive payday it would bring, and that was practically the same thing.

Stella sat there stiff as a board. It was obvious she was trying to keep her mouth shut, but was having a hard time of it. He was sure he could handle her and whatever she threw at him, but it would be nice if he could get in a few more minutes with Frances before she started winding up.

"I'd love to believe that," Frances said.

Stella cleared her throat.

He ignored that, too.

"So, you're saying if you bought the house," Frances said, "you'd want to live here."

"That's what I'm saying."

"But you haven't been back to Christmas Bay since you left after high school, right?"

"You hate Christmas Bay," Stella said flatly. "Why would you live in a town that you hate?"

He held up a hand. "Now, I never said I hate it."

That was also true. He hadn't said it. He'd been thinking it.

"Oh, come on, Ian."

"I have complicated memories of Christmas Bay," he said. "But now that I see it as an adult, it's obviously a great place to raise a family."

Stella made a huffing sound. But Frances's interest seemed piqued.

"Honestly," she said. "I love the idea of someone I know buying the house, over complete strangers…"

He smiled.

"And you really think you'd want to settle down here? It's awfully fast. Or have you been thinking of settling down for a while?"

Stella had been taking a sip of her coffee, but she coughed at that.

"Sorry," she croaked. "Went down the wrong pipe."

Ian narrowed his eyes at her before looking back at Frances. "Oh, you know. For a while now." If he was keeping track, that would go in the whopper column. But it couldn't be helped. She'd painted him into a corner.

"How convenient," Stella muttered under her breath.

"Now, Ian," Frances said. "I'm going to tell you the truth. If you made an offer, I think I'd consider it before I'd consider anything else. But I just can't get past what a change this would be for you, coming from the city. What about your job?"

"Oh, I could work remotely for a while. And I'm used to traveling. That wouldn't be a problem."

"But would you be able to acclimate back into small-town life?"

Ian resisted the urge to shift in his seat. He needed to appear convincing, and squirming around like a fibbing third grader wasn't going to get him anywhere.

"It would be an adjustment," he said. "But I've been wanting to make a change for a while, so…"

Frances nodded thoughtfully. He almost had her, he could feel it. But then again, he'd been expecting it. Ian did this for a living, and he was good at it. Really good. By this afternoon, he'd be on the phone with his office, getting the ball rolling. This should be an easy sale, barring anything popping up with the inspection. But that really didn't matter, either. It was the property he was after, not the house, and he'd pay whatever he had to for it.

He leaned back in his chair, the wicker squeaking obnoxiously under his weight. He felt confident, in control. The guilt that had been plaguing him earlier was tucked away in the farthest corners of his mind, ignored. It was all going to work out exactly how he'd hoped. He'd get a kick-ass piece of land, and Frances, whether she realized it or not, would be better off. Taken care of financially. Sure, she'd hate him in the end, but that was inevitable. He could live with it. He'd lived with a lot worse.

Stella continued to stare at him, her eyes cold.

Under different circumstances, he probably would've asked her out by now. Taken her to the nicest restaurant he could find, and impressed her by ordering the most expensive bottle of wine. If she'd been a stranger, he would've done his damnedest to get her into bed afterward, too. He'd push that dark mane of hair off to the side, and move his lips along her jaw, down her throat. He'd work to get her to look at him the way so many other women did. He might even turn himself inside out for that.

But it was only a fantasy. Because she wasn't a stranger. She'd never liked him before, and she sure as hell didn't like him now. Again, he reminded himself that he didn't care.

Still, as he stared back at her, he knew that deep down, where that sliver of guilt lay, he did care. Just a little. Just enough to swallow hard now, his tongue suddenly feeling thick and dry in his mouth.

Frances took a sip of her coffee. Then another, as the clock ticked from the other room. The cat continued purring on his foot, and he thought his eyes felt itchy now. Or maybe that was just his imagination.

"I know you want the house, Ian," she finally said, setting the coffee cup down again. "And I want you to have the house."

His heart beat evenly inside his chest.

"On one condition..."

He raised his brows. Stella raised hers, too, and looked over at her foster mother. Even the cat, probably sensing the sudden stiffness in Ian's body, shifted and yawned.

"If you're serious about this," she continued, "if you're serious about living in Christmas Bay again, I want you to stay for a couple weeks. Until Christmas Eve."

He stared at her. Stella stared at her, too.

"If you can work remotely," she said, "that shouldn't be a problem. You can get reacquainted with the town, with the people. Stella can show you around and introduce you. Then, you can truly decide if you want to put down some roots here. And if that's how you feel in your heart, I'll be able to tell. I'll be able to see it written all over your face."

Ian felt his mouth go slack. The house—his great investment opportunity, a deal so sure, he'd been writing up the papers in his head—was so quiet you could hear a pin drop. Outside the windows, there was the muted sound of the ocean, the waves slamming against the cliffs of Cape Longing. He felt his pulse tapping steadily in his neck as he let her words, her surprisingly genius condition, settle like a weight in his stomach.

Well, son of a bitch.

He hadn't been expecting *that*.

Stella couldn't stop gaping at Frances. She knew she was doing it. She must've looked like a sea bass, but she couldn't help it. The shock was all-consuming.

Across the room, Ian was apparently just as shocked. He didn't look like a sea bass—unfortunately he was too handsome for that. But he did look like Frances had dropped a sizable bomb right in his lap.

He seemed at a loss for words. Stella couldn't blame him. She was in the same boat.

"I'm sorry," she managed after a minute. "What?"

Frances folded her hands in her lap, her Christmas sweater sparkling in the morning light. This one had a sequined snowman emblazoned on the front.

"You heard me," she said evenly.

Ian glanced over at Stella, and for the first time since he'd arrived, he looked taken aback. She had to hand it to Frances. She'd surprised them both. And she'd done it on her own terms. If she was going to sell the house, she was going to sell it to whomever she chose. She was not a forgetful old lady who couldn't handle her affairs. She could still manage just fine, and she was going to prove it.

Stella felt a distinctive warmth creep into her cheeks. She loved Frances so much, but she realized she'd been coddling her for the last few weeks. Treating her like a child. She stared at her shoes, ashamed.

Still, Ian *staying* here? And having to show him around? It was worse than him just making an outright offer. Much worse.

Taking a deep breath, she settled her gaze on Frances again, this time trying to center herself. "Frances, can we at least talk about this?"

"There's nothing to talk about. I was up half the night thinking about it, and it makes perfect sense."

Ian frowned, clearly wondering how he'd been so close to a deal, only to let this wriggle right out of his grasp. Normally, Stella would be gloating, but she couldn't even bring herself to do that. What a cluster.

"I trust your instincts, Stella," Frances said. "You might think I'm dismissing all your concerns, but it's actually because I've been listening that I'm doing this. By spending time with Ian, you'll be able to gauge his true feelings."

She turned to Ian then. "And I love you to pieces, Ian. I know you probably have a hard time believing that, but I do. However, I need to know you're not just here for the real estate. And this way, I'll know."

Ian swallowed visibly. "Frances..."

"There's really nothing you can say to make me change my mind. It's made up. If you're serious about the house you'll stay, or you won't and I'll find another buyer. It's as simple as that."

Stella watched her foster mother, impressed with her badassery, and at the same time horrified that she appeared to mean everything she'd just said. Ian was going to stay. *Until Christmas Eve.*

That is...unless he didn't. She looked over at him, wondering if Frances had called his bluff. There was always that possibility, and she felt the stirrings of hope in her belly. Maybe she wouldn't have to spend any more time with him, after all.

He seemed deep in thought. His dark brows were furrowed, his jaw working methodically. He looked far away, weighing how much he actually wanted the property, no doubt. Was it really worth two weeks of his life? She guessed he already had more money than God. Why did he need more?

But right as she was thinking it, his gaze shifted to Frances, and there was something in his eyes that told Stella her foster mother might've just met her match.

"It's a deal, Frances," he said evenly. "On Christmas Eve, you'll see that I'm the right buyer for this house."

"I'm still not sure what you mean," Carter said, sounding confused on the other end of the line. "You're *staying* there?"

Ian sighed and leaned back against the motel bed's headrest. There was a light rain falling outside, and the ocean churned, grumpy and gray beyond the beach. He really didn't care to repeat himself—he wasn't in the mood. But the fact was, he was going to have to be doing a lot of that in the days to come. Telling people over and over again why he was here. His associates, his employees, Christmas Bay locals. He swallowed a groan. *God.* The Christmas Bay locals. If the front desk lady was any indication of the amount of nosiness around here, he'd have to tell everyone his business. And would any of them swallow his reasons for wanting to come back here? They'd have to if he had any hope of convincing Frances.

He felt his shoulders tighten. And it wasn't just Frances anymore. It was Stella, too. And having to convince her was what had him worried. Plenty.

"Yes," he said, gripping his phone tighter than he needed to. "It's a long story. But in order to secure this sale, I need to put the time in."

"Yeah, but two *weeks*?"

He could almost see his partner leaning back in her corner office chair, the bay sparkling behind her. She'd think this was ridiculous, of course. She'd think Ian was losing his edge if it was taking him two days to make a sale, much less two weeks. But if he didn't secure it, as far as he was concerned, that *would* be losing his edge, and he wasn't about to let that happen. Two weeks was a long time, but it would be worth it in the end. Another notch in his belt, another win for his company. And his bank account. All he needed was for Carter to take over while he was gone and deal with their clients in person. He could Zoom until the cows came home, but some of them were finicky and needed to be handled like high-strung racehorses. Zoom meetings didn't always cut it.

"Two weeks," Ian said. "Just trust me on this."

"Okaaay. Two weeks. I can't wait to hear all about it."

That was a lie. Carter didn't actually care if Ian camped out on the moon, just as long as he made them money. She was just as cutthroat as he was. Maybe even more so, and that was saying something in this business.

"Listen," Ian said. "I'm going to drive down tomorrow and pick up some clothes. So if you need me for anything, I can swing by the office before heading back. I'll call on the way down, okay?"

"Sounds good. Talk then."

Ian hung up and rubbed his temple. The headache from yesterday had turned into a full-blown pain in the ass. What he really needed to do was get in the car and head to the little market in town. Pick up a few groceries for his room. He had a microwave, minifridge and a coffeepot, thank God. He'd be living on macaroni and cheese and granola bars for a while. *Great.* This really couldn't get much worse.

But it could get worse, he knew that. He could put in the time and effort for this property, and by Christmas Eve, he might not be able to convince Stella that he was being genuine. He might not be able to convince Frances to sell to him, and then what?

He scraped a hand through his hair. He'd just have to cross that bridge when he came to it. Right now, he was going to have to gird his loins and head into town.

Lord help him.

Stella watched seven-year-old Gracie, wearing a pink slicker with the hood flopping on her shoulders, run up the beach.

"Don't go too far!" Kyla yelled through her cupped hands.

At that, Gracie turned and waved. She was so cute. Dark hair, dark eyes. Maybe one of the cutest kids Stella had ever seen. And she was about to get a brand-new stepmom. Kyla was going to marry Ben Martinez, Christmas Bay's police chief and the love of her life, next spring. She was positively glowing.

But as she walked alongside Stella now, the wind blowing her shoulder-length hair in front of her face, she looked more worried than anything.

"I'm not sure I like this," Kyla said. "It has trouble written all over it."

Stella pulled her cardigan tighter around her, watching as Gracie bent down to inspect something in the sand, then shoved it in her slicker pocket. Stella hoped it wasn't alive. "Tell me about it. I haven't liked it from the beginning."

"And this was Frances's idea? Actually, don't answer that. It sounds exactly like something Frances would do."

Stella nodded. "I know. She definitely wants to know Ian's serious, but there's also a part of her that wants to show us she's still in control. I'm proud of her. I mean, I'm super annoyed, but you have to hand it to her. It's kind of brilliant."

"So, what are you going to do?"

"What can I do? The only way to know for sure if Ian's serious is to spend some time with him, like she said. And even then, I'm not sure he'll ever be honest with us. What if he keeps up this charade about wanting to live in the house?"

"Then she'll have to trust you when you tell her it's just a charade."

Stella looked out over the water. It was gorgeous today. A little windy—the ocean was choppy and unsettled—but the sun was out, warming everything up.

"That's true," she said. "But two weeks… It seems like a lifetime."

Kyla hooked her arm in Stella's. "I'm sorry you got stuck with this."

"Me too. But Frances is worth it. The house is worth it. I'll just have to keep reminding myself of that every time I have to be within five feet of him."

Kyla laughed. "He's still that bad?"

"Worse."

"But good-looking."

Stella turned to her. "Who told you that?"

"Frances. On the phone this morning."

"What do his looks have to do with anything?"

"Nothing…but just how good-looking are we talking?"

"Kyla."

Her foster sister shrugged. "I'm just saying, you're single…"

"Gross. He's an ass."

"But a good-looking ass."

Stella raised a hand to shield her eyes from the sun, watching as Gracie drew in the sand with a stick. "I guess."

"Listen, you don't have to do this all by yourself. Ben and I can help. Bring him over for dinner or something. Take him to see Marley and the baby. Really lay it on thick. Maybe he'll decide he's in over his head and will give up. I mean, how much Christmas Bay can a person take, if they hate everything about Christmas Bay?"

Stella contemplated this, her wheels turning. "That's true…"

"I bet after a few days, he'll start wondering what the hell he's doing here and will leave early."

"Kyla," Stella said slowly. "You just gave me the best idea."

"Uh-oh."

"He'd *definitely* have second thoughts if he has a miserable time. Remember when Frances took us crabbing in middle school, and we were all hungry and cold, and Marley ended up falling in the water?"

"The infamous crabbing day. How could I forget?"

Stella smiled. *"Exactly."*

"Are you going to take him to the bay and push him in?"

"Don't tempt me. But why should we have to sugarcoat anything? Living in a small town isn't like a Hallmark movie. There are all kinds of things about it that drive you crazy. I'm just saying, I'll show him around. I'll introduce him to people. With the sole purpose of reminding him why he hated it here to begin with."

"Oh, you are *bad*."

"Not half as bad as he is." Stella lifted her chin as a flock of seagulls squabbled overhead, dipping and bobbing on the chilly breeze. "He dealt the cards," she said. "Now I'll show him I can play."

Chapter Four

Ian stood in the motel's parking lot, waiting for Stella to pick him up. The clock was officially ticking—counting down to Christmas Eve—and she was apparently committed to showing him around, just like Frances wanted. At least, that's what she'd said on the phone this morning, in a clipped, go-to-hell tone.

She was supposed to pick him up at nine, and they'd go to the diner on the highway for breakfast. If memory served, this was the place he'd passed coming into town, and that was exactly what it had said on the sign. *Diner.* He couldn't wait. The food was probably just as underwhelming as the name. He'd made sure to put some antacids in his pocket, expecting to have heartburn by ten.

He craned his neck, looking down the road, not

really knowing what he was looking for. He had no idea what Stella drove. He just had the distinct feeling that she wanted to be in control today. In her own car, on her own turf. That was fine. It didn't matter whose turf they were on—he fully intended to leave here with what he'd come for. She could strap him to her hood, for all he cared.

"Good morning, Mr. Steele!"

He turned to see the front desk lady standing a few yards away. She was carrying a stack of towels, her Christmas tree earrings swinging on either side of her round, softly wrinkled face. *Loretta.* Her name was Loretta. She'd officially introduced herself last night, when he'd come down to the office to rent a movie because he'd been bored out of his skull. She'd gone into a detailed explanation of the meaning of her first name, her middle name and her last name, which was Dwight. She'd also explained that her family was from Tennessee, originally, but that she and her husband had moved out here to be closer to their daughter and grandson, who had terrible asthma.

This, of course, was exactly the kind of conversation that people from the city thought they'd have with people from a small town. But it was what it was, and he'd managed to listen without his eyes glazing over.

So. There was that. He knew way more about Loretta Dwight than he ever cared to. Still, he plastered on a smile now, and nodded hello. Might as well get into character and stay there. Christmas Eve was still a way off.

"Good morning," he said. "How are you?"

He immediately regretted asking. He might be here all day.

"My grandson is a little under the weather this morning," she said. "He's got the beginnings of a cold, and those always go straight to his lungs. But other than that, I'm fine as a frog's hair. Where are you off to looking so handsome this morning?"

Oh, this lady. He couldn't stay annoyed. She was just so open, so honestly friendly, that he felt himself soften toward her, just a little.

"Nowhere exciting," he said. "Just breakfast with a friend."

"Oh?" She winked at him. "A lady friend, maybe?"

She knew he was here for business—she'd gotten that out of him when he'd first checked in. But for some reason, she wanted him to be here for pleasure, too. It was like she couldn't stand for him to be working the whole time—he also needed to be having fun. Apparently with a lady friend.

"Just a friend," he said. That was stretching it. In fact, he was surprised he managed to get that out without choking on it. "Actually, more like an associate." That was better.

"Oh, that sounds important."

Before he could reply, a car pulled up behind him. He looked over his shoulder to see Stella sitting in an old Jeep Wagoneer, its exhaust curling into the cold morning air.

He nodded at Loretta. "Well, here's my ride. Have a good day."

"You too!"

He opened the door and climbed in, nearly bumping his head on the roof.

"Nice suit, Ian," Stella said. "You know we're not going to the Four Seasons, right?"

Yanking the scat belt across his chest, he shot her a look. "It's a blazer and slacks. Sorry I didn't wear my regulation coastal uniform of jeans and a hoodie."

"Ouch. Well, that's one strike against Christmas Bay, then. No fashion sense. Unless, of course, you're completely full of it, and you have zero intention of living here, like you're trying to convince Frances you are."

So, they were going to start sparring right away. He wasn't surprised. Still, he would've liked to get some coffee in him first. Have some caffeine ammunition for that barbed tongue of hers.

"I've never been much of a clothes guy, anyway," he said, leaning back in his seat.

She laughed and put the car into gear. "Riiiight."

"You think I'm shallow?"

"Do you have to ask?"

"Well, I resent that," he said. "Besides, we can't all be as deep as you."

"You don't even know me."

"But I knew you before."

"How deep can a fourteen-year-old be?"

"Deep enough to always make me feel like I was doing something wrong."

"You *were* always doing something wrong."

She had him there. Time to change the subject.

"So, Stella," he said. "Tell me about the adult you. Married? Single? Kids?"

She gave him some side-eye as she turned left onto the highway. "Is this the part where you try to get to know me, so you can manipulate me?"

"Wow."

She didn't respond to that. Just shifted the Jeep into third, her long dark hair concealing her face enough so that he couldn't see her expression.

After a long minute, she sighed. "I'm single."

He waited for her to go on. She was right—he needed to get to know her, and for that to happen, he couldn't push. He needed to manipulate her without her *realizing* he was manipulating her. He really was an ass.

"I guess you could say I've been unlucky in love," she continued.

"Why's that?"

She glanced at him. "You know why. When you grew up like we did…well, I don't trust people. Not a good recipe for relationships."

He let this settle. Every girlfriend he'd ever had

would probably agree with that. It was the theme song to his whole damn life.

Looking out the window, he watched the evergreens zoom by. Every now and then, they'd pass a car going in the opposite direction, but mostly, the highway was empty.

He couldn't help but admire how beautiful it was this morning. The mountains came right to the edge of the ocean, the low clouds wrapping around their peaks like a cloak. The sky was steely, the air tangy with the smell of salt water and pine. Sea birds flew low, barely having to beat their wings, letting the wind carry them where they wanted to go.

Ian pulled in a breath and let it out slowly. Like so many things, he'd forgotten how being this close to nature could make him feel. Calm. Balanced. But before he could feel sentimental about that, he cleared his throat and looked back at Stella.

"Is that why you came back here?" he asked. "Bad relationship?"

"I came back for Frances. Her diagnosis has been worrying us for a while, but her memory has gotten pretty bad lately. She got lost on a walk..."

She let her voice trail off. Maybe realizing who she was talking to. Again, she kept her head turned at an angle where he couldn't see past her hair.

Despite everything, despite still feeling bitter toward Frances for those two years he'd been forced to live with her, he'd never wish memory loss on anyone. It must be awful knowing what was coming, and not being able to do anything about it.

"I'm sorry," he said.

Stella looked over at him, gave him a small smile and looked back at the road again. "She has us. She'll be okay. As long as we can protect her from people who don't have her best interests at heart."

There was no point arguing with that, so he wasn't going to try. They'd be at the diner soon enough, anyway, and maybe the small talk could be kept to a minimum if their mouths were full of food. All of a sudden, he was starving. He realized he hadn't eaten since the previous afternoon. He'd been too busy catching up on work. And then, of course, there'd been the DVD rental when he thought he couldn't take the four beige walls of his motel room one minute longer. He should've gone out for a hamburger instead.

"What about you, Ian?" she asked.

"What about me?"

"What happened to you after leaving Christmas Bay?"

He grit his teeth, staring out the window. Now they were getting into uncomfortable territory. Of course, nothing said he had to tell the truth. He hadn't been telling her much of it so far. But he knew if he had any chance of these next few weeks being worth his time, he needed to humor her. Answer her questions.

Act interested in what she had to say. It was the natural thing to do.

Still, at the thought of those first few tumultuous years after leaving Frances's house, his throat tightened. He didn't talk about his past for a reason.

He gave her what he hoped was an easy smile. "Oh, you know. Drank too much, partied too hard. Tried to figure it out in all the wrong places. Then finally got myself together and managed to finish college. Got lucky with a few sales and investments, and before I knew it, I had my own company." He shrugged. She didn't have to know the dirty details. "The rest is history."

"I know about the trying to figure it out part," she said. "My vice was travel. I went everywhere that wasn't Christmas Bay. Trying to outrun the memories, I guess. Come to peace with what happened to me when I was little."

He watched her. He remembered asking about her past once when they were kids. She'd barely opened up, before shuttering again, which had been exactly Stella's style back then. Still, he'd always felt a connection with her through their shared experience. They'd both had it rough.

"What happened to you?"

She gripped the steering wheel harder at that. Her knuckles actually went white, before she eased up and wiggled her fingers a little.

"I don't think my parents ever really liked me,"

she said. "I mean, I don't think they ever wanted to have me, but there I was. My dad was totally indifferent. He was never around. But my mom…"

She didn't even have to finish that sentence for him to know exactly what she was talking about. He'd also had a mother who'd never liked him.

Stella shrugged, her eyes on the road. "I think she resented me from the beginning. She had me when she was a teenager, so that made it a thousand times harder. She had to grow up too fast, and I was just a constant reminder of what she'd missed out on."

He listened, quiet. His mother hadn't had the excuse of youth to fall back on. She'd just been a genuinely horrible parent from the get-go.

"She was always breaking up and getting back together with my dad. And in between there were boyfriends…"

He swallowed hard. He knew about those, too. There was a time when he'd lost track of all the bruises on his body. He'd eventually used every mark as a promise to himself to leave the first chance he got. And he had. It just hadn't been soon enough.

"Were they abusive?" he asked, his voice low. All of a sudden, he felt a rush of anger that he didn't quite know what to do with. Was it on his behalf? Or Stella's?

"Physically, sometimes," she said. "Most of the time it was emotional, though."

He nodded, remembering those afternoons at the

city pool. Remembering her T-shirts and shorts, and how he'd picked on her about it. Maybe a dark seed had been planted in her psyche back then. Something that made her see herself differently than how everyone else saw her. And he'd made it worse.

He shifted in his seat, not liking the feeling of shame that was trying to creep into his subconscious. He'd been a kid. He hadn't known what the hell she'd been struggling with. Maybe if she'd told him, instead of pushing everyone away all the time, he might've shut up about it.

Deep down, he knew that was no excuse, but it seemed to do the trick. He was able to smother those inconvenient sparks of emotion before they could catch fire and do some real damage. *Cool and detached.* That's how he was going to stay for the next few weeks. And then Stella Clarke would be nothing more than a footnote in his life. Someone he might think of in passing, when he remembered the incredible deal he'd scored on the Cape Longing property.

After another minute or two spent in blessed silence, they finally pulled up to the diner. Ian shifted in his seat, looking at all the cars and trucks in the gravel parking lot. Apparently, the simple little diner with the blinking neon sign on its roof was the place to be on a weekday morning. Didn't these people work?

Stella parked the Jeep underneath a massive pine tree that was probably going to drip sap all over it, but he kept his mouth shut. The last time he'd parked underneath a tree had been in college when he'd driven an Accord. When you drove a Porsche, tree sap and bird crap were the mortal enemy. Just another thing he'd have to get used to in the coming weeks. There weren't exactly any parking garages in Christmas Bay.

Turning the engine off, she took off her seat belt. "Hope you're hungry," she said. "Best biscuits and gravy around."

He hadn't had biscuits and gravy for almost as long as he'd avoided parking underneath trees, but whatever. His low-carb diet, his strict gym routine, his habit of being the best-dressed man in the room, were all going to have to take a back seat for the time being. If eating like a local was going to help him fit in, at least in Stella's and Frances's eyes, well, then he'd just have to tuck his napkin into his collar and get down to business.

"Starving," he said, winking at her.

She rolled her eyes.

They got out, and he walked behind her, forcing himself to keep his gaze off her backside. It wasn't easy, though. She wore a faded pair of Levi's that hugged her in all the right places. Her dark hair tumbled down her back, and he thought he could smell her shampoo on the salty breeze. Her sweater was oversize and chunky, definitely nothing to write home about, but he found himself wondering what she looked like underneath.

He reached out and opened the door for her. She kept her eyes averted, carefully avoiding touching him as she passed.

Inside, they stood behind a Please Wait To Be Seated sign, and Ian glanced around. It was like one of those movies where the outsider walks into a café, and everyone stops talking all at once.

He immediately felt squirmy underneath their curious gazes, and resisted the urge to look down at his clothes. He wasn't *that* dressed up, just business casual. No, they were staring because this was a small town, and he had the gall to be new.

Beside him, Stella smiled innocently. "Regulars," she said. "You stick out."

Probably what she'd been hoping for. Actually, *exactly* what she'd been hoping for, he'd put money on it.

He smiled back. So, she was going to dish it out. That was okay, he could take it. He'd take it all the way to the bank.

They watched each other for a long minute. Ian wasn't going to break eye contact first. It was childish, but something about this woman made him feel like a teenager again. He couldn't decide yet if that was a good thing, or a bad thing.

"Hey, girl!"

They both startled at the sound of the voice coming from behind the pickup counter. Ian looked over to see a man in his twenties waving enthusiastically in their direction. He was wearing a hairnet and an apron with a giant Santa Claus on it that said Santa Baby! He'd obviously come from the kitchen.

"You weren't going to come in without saying hi, were you?" he said.

"Hey, Henry!" Stella said. "I wasn't sure you'd be working today."

"Aww, hon. I work every day." The man, Henry apparently, turned his attention to Ian. He looked him up and down, before grinning wide. "Well, now. Who's this?"

Stella glanced up at Ian, a twinkle in her eyes. "This is Ian," she said. "Ian Steele. He's thinking about making an offer on Frances's house."

"Is he now?"

"He's from Christmas Bay originally, but left after high school, so he's going to spend a few weeks here first. See if he likes it. Or at least gets used to it again."

"Honey. What's not to like?"

"Well, you know it's fabulous, and I know it's fabulous, but he's been away a long time. He might not acclimate very well from the city…"

Ian shifted on his feet, completely aware that Stella had the home court advantage here, and she wanted him to feel as uncomfortable as possible. If that meant taking him to every greasy spoon in town, he had a feeling that was exactly what she was going to do.

"Ian," Stella said sweetly. "This is my friend Henry."

Henry waved. "Hi, there. And don't listen to Stella. I'm sure you'll acclimate just fine. We're all a pretty friendly bunch. Nobody bites. That I'm aware of."

Stella laughed.

"How do you two know each other?" Ian asked.

"We do yoga together at Water Street Gym," Henry said. "I critique her downward dog, and she gives me relationship advice. Win-win."

"There's nothing wrong with my downward dog," Stella said.

"There's nothing wrong with it *now.*" Henry winked at her. "Well, I'd better get back to it. There's an omelet back there with my name on it. It was good to see you, hon. And it was nice meeting you, Ian."

"You too."

"And good luck with the house," Henry said. "I don't care what Stella says, I think you'd fit in great."

And with that, he turned on his heel and disappeared into the kitchen.

Stella watched him go, looking slightly annoyed.

"What's the matter?" Ian said. "You were expecting him to take your side?"

"Maybe."

"If you think you're going to introduce me to your buddies, and they're all going to hate me because

I'm new, think again. I was born and raised here, too, remember?"

She glared up at him. "Henry loves everyone. But if he knew you better, he wouldn't be able to stand you, either."

"Don't beat around the bush or anything."

At that, she turned to face him, her chin raised slightly. There was fire in her eyes. "Just for the record, I think showing you around is a terrible idea. But Frances seems to want to give you a chance, so I'm doing it for her. But you're kidding yourself if you think I'm going to let my guard down around you for one second. I don't trust you as far as I can throw you."

He smiled down at her. "I'm glad you feel like you can be honest with me."

"I don't care."

"Now, see? It seems like you do care. A lot."

"About Frances."

"And maybe about me, too."

She laughed. "Right."

"Admit it. We've got chemistry. That's not a bad thing. In fact, you could use it to your advantage."

"Are you serious?"

"Very."

"Is that how the women in your orbit work? They have to play you?"

He shook his head. "No, they simply know how to handle me. And I know how to handle them. It is what it is."

"Is there *any* genuine bone in your body?"

He shrugged.

"So, what you're saying is, I should lean into this *chemistry* we've got—" she used air quotes around the word *chemistry* "—and I might be able to get you to leave Frances's house alone?"

"I didn't say that."

"Then what are you saying?"

"I'm simply reminding you that we could work together. You can tell Frances I only have good intentions for the house, and you could see her financially set. I'd think that would make you happy."

"I told you, it's not about the money."

"And I told you, she's going to need it. You have to know that, Stella."

"Stop acting like you care about her, Ian. You only care about yourself."

"You really don't know anything about me."

"I know you haven't seen your aunt in years."

Well, damn.

He stared down at her. So, Christmas Bay was even smaller than he thought. Still, it was surprising that she knew about this, when literally nobody in his life knew. He never talked about his family, distant or otherwise.

"Yeah," she continued. "That's right. And she's a nice lady, too. I have a friend who works at Weatherly Court. It didn't take long to connect the dots. So, I know that once upon a time, you had some people here who cared about you. And you washed your hands of her, just like you washed your hands of Frances and this entire town when you left it."

He smiled slowly, forcing down the anger that threatened to choke him where he stood. Nobody in Ian's professional life had the guts to challenge him much. And when it came to his personal life, nobody knew enough to challenge him, period. He didn't like how that felt. He didn't like the accusation, because it held a sliver of truth to it. Maybe more than a sliver.

"Well done," he said, his voice smooth as scotch. "You're not only beautiful, but you're clever as hell. You're a formidable opponent, Stella Clarke."

She swallowed visibly and looked away. He'd unsettled her. Stella's vulnerability had always been her looks, and he wasn't above using that to his advantage.

"Table for two?" They both turned to see a server standing there, eyeing them awkwardly. "Unless... Do you need a minute?"

Ian felt a distinct heat creep up his neck. He'd almost forgotten they were in a public place. Who knows how many people had heard them just now? And by the looks of it, Stella had forgotten, too. Her cheeks had turned bright pink in a matter of seconds.

"Oh...uh..." she stammered.

"No," Ian said, stepping forward. "We're ready. Aren't we?"

She nodded, avoiding eye contact with him completely.

They followed the server to a little table in the corner. Something intimate and quiet. She probably thought they were a couple, and why wouldn't she? They'd been arguing just now like they were about to scratch each other's eyes out, or jump into bed.

He guessed what he'd said about their chemistry was true.

Now, he just had to figure out what to do about it.

Chapter Five

Stella unlocked the front door of Coastal Sweets, looking out the window to the tourists walking by on the sidewalk. Only a couple more weeks to shop until Christmas, and they weren't wasting a single second. It was a beautiful Saturday morning for it, too. Sunny and crisp, without much wind. A rarity for Christmas Bay in December.

Behind her, Frances tinkered with the vintage cash register on the counter.

"I think we might have to get Allen to come out here and take a look at this thing," she said. "The drawer is sticking again."

"Or maybe we should just get a new one, Frances. Step into the new millennium, twenty years late?"

Frances made a tsking sound. "What's the fun in that? This is a classic."

Stella turned around and smiled at her. She, Kyla and Marley had found that cash register at Earl's Antiques down the street, and had bought it for Frances's fiftieth birthday. She was ridiculously proud of it. Stella knew she'd probably never get rid of it, even if she had to use a crowbar to pry the drawer open from here on out.

"You're absolutely right," she said. "It is a classic."

"It's just like the house, honey. It's got character, history. My very favorite things."

Stella nodded, leaning against the counter. Beauregard was in his princess bed this morning, making biscuits next to the cash register in question. Frances had had to post a sign next to him that said Please Don't Feed the Cat Jelly Beans. They Upset His Tummy. The things you had to address when little kids were 90 percent of your clientele.

"Speaking of the house," Frances said, reaching over to scratch Beauregard behind the ears. "How'd it go yesterday? Kyla said you took Ian out to breakfast?"

Stella's stomach tightened. She'd been trying to put Ian out of her mind all morning, without much success. And she couldn't really figure out why. She couldn't stand the guy. She'd even told him so, straight to his face.

But the thing was, she could also tell there was

more to Ian Steele than met the eye. A lot of that was worse than met the eye…but not all of it. And that was the part that had her unsettled. Despite his super polished exterior, there was something underneath that was much rawer. She could see it in his eyes sometimes, right before they shuttered completely. She'd seen it yesterday when she'd mentioned his aunt. And she'd seen it again when she'd dropped him off at his motel, when he'd turned to say something, but had stopped himself short.

So he was more of a mystery than she'd expected. Which made it hard to look her foster mother in the eyes now, and tell her that she still didn't trust him. That she still didn't want him to buy the house, which he probably had no intention of living in.

Frances gazed at her, and there was no denying the slightly hopeful look on her face. Even with the memory loss, she was still her usual shrewd and pragmatic self. But it was also clear there was a part of her that wanted this to work out. Under any other circumstance, with any other person but Ian, Stella would feel the same way. It was romantic. A man who longed to come home again. But the thing was, it wasn't true. At least that Stella could see.

She licked her lips, wishing one of those shop-happy tourists would walk through their door and interrupt this conversation altogether.

But nobody walked in, and Frances kept waiting patiently for an answer.

"It was okay," Stella finally said. "I took him to the diner on ninety-nine."

"Oh, Lord. Where Henry works?"

"The one and only."

Frances rubbed Beauregard's ears, while seeming to contemplate this. The cat was purring so loud, anyone walking in off the street would assume he was in respiratory distress.

"Well, what did he say?" Frances asked. "Are you getting a better idea of how he feels about the house?"

"I think he's just trying to charm you, Frances. It's a great investment opportunity, and of course, he knows that better than anyone. But…"

"But, what?"

Frances was looking at her so intently. Stella didn't relish the thought of giving Ian even the slightest benefit of the doubt, but her foster mother deserved the truth. After all, that was what this whole two weeks was all about.

"But," Stella finally said, "I do feel like there's something else. A reason why he's here, that maybe he doesn't even know yet. Or maybe that's just my imagination. Trying to read something into this that isn't there."

But even as she said it, she knew that wasn't the case. There was something. She just didn't know what yet.

Frances smiled. "No. I feel it, too."

Right then, the little bell over the candy shop door

tinkled, and they turned to see a couple of teenage girls walk in.

"Welcome!" Frances said enthusiastically.

And Stella knew that she was off the hook, at least for the time being. She might have a hard time getting Ian out of her head this morning, but at least Frances would be distracted from asking any more questions.

At the moment, she had enough questions of her own.

Ian walked out of the convenience store with his arms full of groceries. Technically, they consisted of microwave dinners and junk food, but whatever. They would keep him alive until Christmas, when he could get the hell out of Dodge.

The wind coming off the beach was cold this evening, and he was glad he'd packed his Patagonia ski jacket when he'd driven down for clothes.

Walking across the parking lot, he dug the key fob from his pocket and hit the unlock button. The Porsche chirped twice, its lights blinking through the dusky light. A couple getting out of a battered pickup truck glanced over at the car, then at him. If you were someone living paycheck to paycheck, he guessed the Porsche might be obnoxious. Actually, the Porsche was pretty obnoxious, anyway, but Ian wasn't used to denying himself creature comforts. Until now, that is.

He missed San Francisco. He missed his condo.

He missed his office and the way he picked up his coffee every day from the local bistro on Market Street that roasted their beans in-house. And for the tenth time in the last forty-eight hours, he thought about giving up this ridiculous charade of buying Frances's house to live in, and just going back to where he belonged. There would be other properties, other deals. And besides, it wasn't like he was hurting for the cash.

But every time he felt tempted to leave, he thought about that amazing view. The widow's walk. The staircase that wound three stories up and reminded him of something out of a gothic novel. And he thought about Stella Clarke. The girl from his past who'd grown up to be so beautiful, he had a hard time keeping his eyes off her. Even knowing how she felt about him. Which, if he was being honest with himself, was starting to get to him. He wasn't a terrible person because he saw this situation as advantageous. It wasn't like he was pushing Frances off a cliff or anything. He was simply going to give her a lot of money for her house and move on.

Still, as he slid into his car's buttery leather seats, there was that feeling of guilt again. Why, he had no idea. He'd never had a problem with guilt before. The fact that he was dealing with it now was annoying. More than annoying. It was actually infuriating.

Starting the engine, he leaned his head back against the seat and looked toward the ocean in the distance.

Ever since yesterday when Stella had mentioned his aunt Betty, he'd been thinking about the woman who'd taken him in after he'd run away from Frances's house. She'd been tender and kind, telling him that she'd tried getting custody of him before, but it had been complicated, taking a long time to get through the red tape of the system.

Ian had never believed her, of course. She hadn't *really* wanted him, just like his parents had never wanted him. What was to want? He'd been nothing but an inconvenience, a leech, sucking them dry. That's what he'd been told his entire childhood. Why would he believe this woman he barely knew? Even so, she'd never stopped trying when it came to Ian. Always doing things like getting up every morning to make him a hot breakfast before school. Coming to his basketball games—even though he'd eventually been kicked off the team for stealing a pack of cigarettes from the convenience store down the street from the athletic center. She'd even defended him to the principal, who'd never like Ian, and honestly, had every right.

And what did he do to thank her? He hadn't even said a proper goodbye when he'd left.

Grinding his teeth together, he frowned. Why had he done that? Why had he been so callous? So unfeeling? He knew the answer to that. It was just easier that way. Much easier than letting love in, and letting it hurt you in the end.

He lifted his head off the seat and put the car into Drive. And without allowing any more thoughts into his brain, he drove out of the parking lot slowly, looking both ways before pulling out.

But he didn't turn right, toward the motel. He turned left instead, along the coastline, toward Christmas Bay's small downtown area. Where Frances's candy shop on Main Street was. Where the city hall and fire department were. Where the bundled-up tourists would be walking, even now, with everything closed up for the evening, because that's just how Christmas Bay was. People came here for the beauty of the outdoors, and walks in the evening didn't necessarily have to lead anywhere.

Ian shifted into third as he passed the Christmas tree in Sandpiper Park, where he'd played as a kid. And then he passed the brewery, and the Safeway, with all the weekly specials plastered on the windows.

He swallowed hard as he realized where he was going. Driving straight toward the retirement home where he knew his aunt was living. He knew, because despite what Stella thought, he hadn't forgotten about her. He'd kept tabs on her over the years. Without her knowing, without ever mentioning it to anyone.

He had absolutely no intention of stopping. Of going inside to see her. The thought of that nearly made him sick. There would have to be explanations involved with that. Apologies made. Forgiveness asked. And Ian wasn't going to do any of those things. He simply felt the uncontrollable urge to drive by. To see the place for himself, and make sure... Make sure of what?

He rubbed the stubble on his chin as the sign for Weatherly Court came into view. It was the only retirement home in the area, and it had always been nice. And now, he could clearly see that it had been built onto. According to the sign out front, there was an assisted living portion, as well as memory care. The lights in the original, two-story building glowed warmly through the evening. Outside, a woman walked her fluffy white poodle, its tail like a cotton ball waving in the air.

Ian slowed the Porsche, and the engine softened to a purr. A man looked over from the sidewalk, staring at the car as it glided past, unable to blend into the night. But all Ian could think about, despite trying his hardest to make his mind go blessedly blank, was his aunt in there. He wondered if she had a nice apartment. He wondered if she'd had anyone to help her move in, or if anyone came to visit. He wondered if she was happy or sad. Sick or well. Content or lonesome.

He watched the building get smaller and smaller, and then watched it fade away in the rearview mirror. It was like a metaphor for his life in Christmas Bay.

And how so long ago, he'd let the entire town just fade away, too.

* * *

Day two. Stella looked over at Ian in the passenger's seat of her Jeep and pulled in a breath. Well, technically, he'd been checked into the Jingle Bell Inn for a few days, pretending to care about Frances and her future since he'd arrived. But it was only the second day Stella was having to spend with him. And she wondered how she'd managed to survive this long.

Glancing up from his phone, he looked around. "Here already? I'm almost done..."

Whatever he'd been doing for the last twenty minutes, he'd been lost to the world. *Work*, he'd just told her when she'd picked him up. *Just a Zoom that I need to sit in on.*

He was wearing thick, black-framed glasses this morning that matched his hair perfectly. She could see, as she pulled up to the curb in front of Coastal Sweets, how he probably looked when he went into the office every day. She imagined him in an expensive suit and leather loafers. A crisp, white shirt, the starched collar contrasting against the tanned skin of his neck. He probably looked like a GQ model on those high-rise office days. Not too far removed from the slacks and collared shirt that he wore this morning.

She put the Jeep into Park, feeling the heater blow against her face, and sneaked another glance in his direction.

He glanced back and raised his brows. "What?"

"Nothing."

"Lie."

She pointed to his phone. "Aren't you on your Zoom?"

"I'm muted now. And no camera."

"Ahh."

"You think I'm overdressed again, don't you?"

"I never said that."

"But you're thinking it."

"I'm thinking a lot of things."

"If you knew how soft this shirt was, how good it felt on my skin, you wouldn't be so judgy."

She smiled at that. "You're right. I'm sorry." She reached out and felt the sleeve. And then felt his muscled bicep underneath. *Good Lord.* Her cheeks warmed and she quickly pulled her hand back.

"See?" he said. "Now you know."

Desperate to divert his attention, just in case he'd been able to read her mind, she nodded toward his phone.

"So, what's the meeting about?"

"Zoning laws in Newport Beach. Pretty boring, really."

After another minute, he clicked out of the meeting and shifted to put his phone in his pocket.

"Who are we seeing this morning?" he asked. "I forget."

"Marley," Stella said, unsnapping her seat belt. "She just had a baby."

"Ahh. And she's working in the candy shop?"

"She helps Frances out sometimes. There's a crib in the back, and she comes and goes. But she's actually the announcer for the Tiger Sharks here in Christmas Bay," Stella said with the familiar swell of pride that she always felt when talking about Marley's job.

"The announcer?" Ian asked. "She calls the games?"

She nodded.

"That's very cool. I remember her being a baseball fanatic."

"She was. Still is."

"I guess she'd have to be."

"But she's an even better mom. And you should see Frances with this baby, it's…"

Stella let her voice trail off when she realized she was starting to tell him things that were close to her heart. Family things. Ian wouldn't care about how Frances was with the baby. Or how the baby adored her nana. Even at one month old, Emily's eyes lit up when Frances leaned over to pick her up. It had been love at first sight for both of them. And Stella cherished the moments she got to witness, because just like her foster sisters, she hadn't had a grandmother growing up. Nobody to pinch her cheeks, or make sugar cookies for her, or who smelled like rose petals and lotion. It was all very sweet, very tender, and she hadn't meant to go there with someone who wouldn't be able to understand any of it.

But instead of looking uninterested, Ian appeared exactly the opposite. He'd turned in his seat, so he was facing her, his gaze intent and deep. It was the first time she'd ever seen him look like this, and it unsettled her. She kept thinking she'd seen everything Ian had to offer. And then, just like she'd told Frances, he'd surprise her with some little moment that made her think maybe, just maybe, she might be misjudging him.

Or maybe he was just that manipulative.

"It's what?" he said.

"Mmm?"

"How Frances is with the baby. It's what?"

She licked her lips, feeling herself warm under that gaze. The one that could be so cool sometimes, like the coastal winter itself. But right now, it wasn't cool. It was different—not necessarily warm, but… different.

"It's just sweet," she said quietly. "To see someone like her embracing grandmotherhood like this. Since she could never have kids of her own, and wouldn't have had a family at all, if she and Bud hadn't opened their doors to complete strangers like they did."

He remained still. Taking that in. Taking her in.

She clasped her hands in her lap and glanced away, unable to look into his eyes another second longer, without feeling like she might lose herself in them. Which was ridiculous, but that's how she felt. There was a strange magnetism inside the Jeep that was making the blood rush in her ears.

"That baby's lucky," Ian said after a minute. His voice sounded hoarse, like he was fighting a cold off.

Frowning, she glanced back over.

"I remember how it was not to have anyone," he continued. "And I remember how my aunt made me feel safe. Even though I fought it. I fought it like hell."

Stella sat there, a distinct warmth settling into her bones. She didn't want to trust it, because she didn't trust Ian. But it still felt good to sit there and talk like this.

"Well," he continued, clearing his throat. "She's lucky to have a grandmother who cares about her so much."

"Can I ask you something?"

"Shoot."

"If your aunt made you feel safe, why haven't you come back to see her since you left?"

She knew that as difficult as Ian had been during his time with Frances, and as pompous as he came across as a grown man, he'd experienced real trauma in his childhood. But she couldn't understand why he was still turning his back on someone who cared about him.

Stella was just the opposite. She couldn't say she wasn't jaded, she absolutely was. And she was hesitant to let people in. But when she let herself love, she loved deeply. She didn't think she would've been able to walk away from genuine kindness as easily as Ian had. It bothered her. She wanted to know why.

Maybe if she knew why, she might get to know him better. And the better she knew him, the better off Frances would be.

He looked down at his hands, and the muscles in his jaw bunched. She got the distinct feeling that he was deciding whether or not to answer.

But then, his gaze met hers again, and she knew he was going to. Whether or not it would be the truth was anyone's guess, but he was going to placate her with something.

"I never used to let myself think about her," he said. "Because when I thought about her, when I let those feelings in, others came with them. And I never wanted to deal with those."

She nodded slowly. She understood that.

"And now?" she asked.

"Now? I still don't want to deal with them."

She eyed him. He had to know that wasn't what she wanted to hear. Especially since he said he wanted to move back to Christmas Bay and establish a new life here. Wouldn't he have to deal with those feelings sooner, rather than later?

"That doesn't mean I won't," he added quickly. He smiled, and it was almost too perfect. Too charming. "Being back here will be the perfect opportunity to mend old fences, and all that."

She leaned away, annoyed that she'd let herself get sucked in. Remembering that Ian was only here for Ian. Nothing else.

"Sure," she said. "Right."

"You don't believe me?"

"Not really."

"That's too bad."

They sat there for a minute, the winter sun shining in through the Jeep's windows. It was golden and warm through the glass, and made Ian's eyes look paler than they'd been before.

And again, she found herself wondering if anything he ever said was true.

Chapter Six

Ian walked through the door of the little candy shop, the bell tinkling above his head, and breathed in the scent that took him right back to his freshman year of high school. He'd come in regularly during the time he'd lived with Frances. All her foster kids had. She'd handed out free candy, after all. Who wouldn't?

But he'd come in before that, too. When he'd been little and his mother hadn't been so messed up yet. When she'd cared about things like getting her son a fistful of Tootsie Pops, his favorite.

He looked around now, trying to ignore the strange feeling sitting in the middle of his chest. It wasn't quite nostalgia, and it wasn't quite sadness. It was somewhere in between. The store looked exactly as it had fifteen years ago. Maybe a little more worn around the edges, but basically the same. The bins sparkled, and the hardwood floor gleamed in the morning light. He remembered Frances always sweeping, or wiping something down. And she was obviously still as meticulous about the place as she ever was.

But the woman standing behind the counter wasn't the woman who'd welcomed him into her home all those years ago. This woman was curvy and blonde, and had a sleeping baby in a soft carrier strapped to her chest.

When she saw him, she smiled wide. Even if he hadn't already known this was Marley, he would've remembered her eyes, and that smile. Not that she'd smiled a ton back then, but when she had, it had lit up the room.

"Well, Ian Steele," she said. "I can hardly believe it."

He smiled back. "How are you, Marley?"

"Busy," she said, nodding toward the baby's downy head resting against her chest. "I've been so busy, but it's worth it. I think the question is, how are *you*?"

Ian crossed his arms over his chest, feeling Stella's watchful gaze on him. This outing was a test, of course, a continuation of this epic battle of wills they had going on, so it was imperative that it go well. Thankfully, he'd always liked Marley. What he'd known of her, at least. It wouldn't be hard to pretend he was glad to see her. What took him off guard, though, was there was a part of him that really *was* glad to see her. He hadn't been expecting that.

"I'm doing well," he said. "I'm sure you know why I'm here?"

Marley nodded, and glanced over at her foster sister. "Oh, I know. Stella filled me in."

"Well, don't believe everything she says. I'm not the devil incarnate."

Stella shot him a look.

But if Marley thought he was as bad as Stella did, she didn't let on. Instead, she began unbuckling the baby carrier with a warm expression on her face.

"I'm glad you're here," she said matter-of-factly. "I need a break from carrying this munchkin around. Will you take her for a minute while I stretch my back?"

Ian stared at her. He didn't do babies. Ever. Like, *ever*, ever. He didn't have a reason to. His life was completely sanitized, just the way he liked it. And kids weren't exactly sanitary.

He shook his head. "Oh, no. I couldn't…"

"Sure you could."

Ian grit his teeth. Maybe this was part of the test. Maybe Marley, as innocent-looking as she was, was in on it, too. They were probably all in on it.

"Oh, come on," Marley said. "Haven't you ever held a baby before?"

The answer to that was a definitive no. Jill had brought her infant nephew into the office once, and handed him around to everyone's collective *oohs* and *aahs*. Ian had made himself scarce, closing his office door before she could suggest he take a turn. He could never understand the obsession over babies. People acted like they were puppies. And he could never understand those, either. Talk about a life complication. And a messy, noisy one, too.

But as he stood there with Stella eyeing him so closely, racking up any and all points against him, he thought about Frances's house, and he forced a deep breath. This was actually a great opportunity to paint himself in the family-man light he was trying so hard to pitch. And if he could get Marley on his side? Well, then. Even better.

He rubbed the back of his neck. "I haven't held one before, I'm sorry to say. I'm used to being around older kids." *Lie. You really are going to hell, Steele.* "But I guess there's no time like the present."

How bad could it be? The baby, who was wearing a red Christmas onesie, was sound asleep and looked about as menacing as a bag of flour. Ian made multimillion-dollar deals every month—he could handle one little baby.

Marley walked out from behind the counter and gently placed the little girl in his arms.

"It's okay," she said. "Just relax. You look scared to death."

"I do?"

"You're not going to break her. But if this makes

you too uncomfortable, you don't have to hold her. I just thought you might like to."

Ian opened his mouth to say something, but found he had no words. No smart reply, nothing suave or debonair. And he simply couldn't push another lie past his vocal cords. Marley had him right where she wanted him. They all did. Another win for Stella.

"You're doing great," Marley said, reaching out to stroke her daughter's hair. "I think you're a natural, Ian."

He took a deep breath and then another as the baby began stirring against his chest. She was warm and soft, and smelled like baby shampoo and fabric softener. She barely weighed anything at all, but that small weight felt so significant right then that he felt his throat constrict.

Ian was used to hearing ego-stroking compliments. People said he was good-looking, that he was charming, that he was smart, confident, capable. The list went on and on. But he'd never heard someone say he was a natural at holding a baby, of all things.

Across the room, Stella greeted a customer and began chitchatting about the weather.

Suddenly, it felt like a private moment between him and Marley. And the little baby, whose eyes had fluttered open a second ago. She was now staring up at him in complete and total wonder.

"You seem surprised," Marley said. "Nobody's ever told you you're good with kids before?"

"Not exactly."

"Maybe nobody's ever taken the time to notice."

Nobody had noticed, because nobody had ever seen him with kids before. Despite what he'd told her so casually a minute ago.

He swallowed with some difficulty. When had he started developing such an annoying conscience, anyway?

"So, you're here to make an offer on Frances's house," Marley said. "And you'll be here until Christmas Eve?"

"That's the plan."

"What are you doing for Christmas? Going back to San Francisco?"

The baby began fussing in his arms. He bounced her up and down.

"Um…yeah," he said.

"I bet it's beautiful there at Christmas. But not as pretty as here." She smiled. "We have the Flotilla of Lights, remember?"

Ian's head began to swim. He'd forgotten about the Flotilla, and how much Frances had loved it. He'd be expected to go, of course. To partake in the festivities and seal the deal, so to speak. A few days ago, that might've felt like just another something he had to get through. But now, it felt more like a lie. And he couldn't understand how that had happened.

The baby began crying in earnest. Then she hiccupped, screwed up her little face and spit up all over him. He'd never seen so much liquid come out of something so small in his entire life.

"Oh, no!" Marley reached out and took her daughter, clearly mortified. "I'm *so* sorry."

"It's okay. Don't worry about it." At least he wasn't wearing one of his Armani suits.

"Ooohhh," Stella said, walking up behind him. "Yikes."

He turned to see that, unlike her foster sister, she didn't look mortified at all. In fact, she looked downright pleased.

"Are you enjoying this?" he asked evenly.

"No. Yes. Maybe a little."

"Good to know."

"I just think it might be some karmic payback."

"For?"

"For waltzing back into town like you own the place."

"I don't own the place. Yet."

"I'm going to go put her down," Marley said, ignoring their banter. She was in full mom mode. "And I'll get you some club soda for your shirt."

"Thanks."

"Be right back."

The customers who'd been browsing the candy bins a minute before had left without buying anything. Now he and Stella were alone. No Marley and her sweet but fussy baby to act as a buffer. And if there was something Ian would've given anything for right then, it was a buffer. Stella and her ever-knowing gaze were doing nothing for his mood.

"Don't worry," she said. "The club soda will get that right out. But you might smell like sour milk until we can get you back to the motel to change."

"Perfect."

"So…I have a busy week planned for you."

"Do tell."

"I thought we could go to Gracie's Christmas pageant this week…"

"Who's Gracie?"

"Ben's daughter."

"Who's Ben?"

"Our police chief. And Kyla's fiancé. Soon-to-be husband."

He nodded. "Got it."

"Then, I thought we might go fishing with Owen. He loves fishing."

"Who's Owen?"

"Marley's boyfriend. Probably soon-to-be fiancé."

"What's with everyone getting married around here?"

Stella smiled. "They're in love. What's wrong with that?"

"Nothing. Nothing's wrong with it."

"You're just not the marrying kind…"

"I didn't say that."

"Of course not, because you're still trying to get

us to buy this crap you're peddling about settling down someday soon."

He leaned against the counter, looking her straight in her lovely eyes. "Speaking of, how am I doing?"

"On peddling your crap?"

"On getting you to see the real me."

"Are you being serious now, or are we just arguing to argue?"

"I'm being very serious."

Something in her expression told him she was actually thinking it over. She was being serious, too.

"Am I as bad as you thought?" he asked, his voice low.

"Honestly?" she said. "Yes and no."

"How's that?"

She grazed her bottom lip with her teeth. She probably hadn't meant for that to be seductive, but it was, anyway, and he had a hard time not leaning closer to her. Which would be kind of like trying to cozy up to a honey badger.

"Sometimes I think I've got you figured out," she said. "I feel like I know what you're thinking and what your motives are. I mean, I think I'm pretty close, anyway."

"And other times?"

"Other times… I'm not sure."

He smiled his most charming smile. "So, you're saying I'm *not* the devil incarnate."

She laughed softly, and she looked so young right

then. Young and sweet, with her whole life in front of her. But the thing was, neither one of them was that young anymore. And they definitely weren't that sweet. Between them, they'd seen too much, experienced too much, to ever be that carefree again.

"I wouldn't go that far," she said, her eyes still twinkling. "But maybe you're not as bad as I was thinking."

He could hardly believe it. He had no idea what he'd done to get her to warm up to him the slightest bit, but whatever it was, it had worked. But he couldn't quite bring himself to be proud of it. He couldn't enjoy this small victory, not knowing how he'd achieved it.

Maybe if he was just deceiving Stella, it might be different. But he wasn't just deceiving Stella, he was deceiving her entire family. Mostly, it would be Frances who would be hurt by this. And yes, he still believed he'd be handing her a very important gift by giving her so much cash for her house. But she'd still be hurt in the end.

He thought of his aunt right then, and wondered how hurt she'd been when he'd left. And then hadn't come back. She was at the end of her life, and she had nobody. Least of all Ian.

Stella frowned, watching him. "What is it?"

Reaching over, he tapped a bobblehead doll of Elvis that sat beside the cash register. It immediately started gyrating, plastic microphone in hand. "Who's the Elvis fan?" he asked.

"You're not going to tell me what you were thinking just now?"

"No."

"Why not?"

"I told you. I try not to go there."

"Any place with feelings?"

"Any place with unpleasant feelings."

"Life can't all be sunshine and rainbows, Ian."

"I know that. I think you and I both know that better than most."

She appeared to let that settle for a few seconds. Then nodded toward the ridiculous little doll that was still swaying back and forth. "I got that in Graceland the summer before last. I saved my tips and paychecks for a couple of years and went on a cross-country road trip. I've always wanted to go to Graceland. I love Elvis."

He could barely remember what it was like to save for something he wanted, and for so long, at that. If he wanted something, he just went out and bought it, and that was that. He had no idea what Stella made waiting tables over the years, but it couldn't be a ton.

"That's impressive," he said. "Did you go on this trip by yourself?"

"I did."

"Wasn't that kind of lonely?"

She shrugged. "Sometimes it was. But mostly, it

was liberating. I got to drive with the windows down and listen to Elvis and think. I did a lot of thinking."

"What did you think about?"

"Everything. My past, my future. My parents and how I never want to be like them. I thought about Frances and how wonderful she is, and about all the memories she gave me here."

"Memories in her house…"

"Yes. The house."

He tapped the bobblehead doll again, and it wiggled back and forth. "You know, that article is coming out next week," he said. "I wonder if people will finally shut up about it being haunted."

"I don't think they'll ever stop talking about that. It's too romantic. But it will definitely stop fanning the flames. It'll be interesting to see how much interest it generates…"

For a few seconds, they'd slipped into a strange kind of camaraderie. And he, for one, had almost forgotten why he was here in the first place. For him, it didn't matter how much interest the article drummed up. It had only been a way to get his foot in the door.

She looked up at him, her eyes suddenly guarded. Gone was the warmth from a minute before. "What happens if someone outbids you, Ian? Or if I don't end up believing what you're trying to sell us?"

"That's just a risk I'm willing to take," he said evenly. "And nobody is going to outbid me."

"It must be nice being so wealthy."

"It has its perks."

"I'm sure it does." She frowned, looking slightly annoyed. "It's none of my business, anyway."

Silence settled over them, as Marley talked softly to the baby in the back room. She must've been having a hard time getting her to go down. The shop was quiet. Too quiet. Tourists were walking by on the sidewalk, but nobody had ventured in again, leaving him alone with this woman, whose judgment was a weight that was getting harder and harder to bear.

Ian felt the muscles in his shoulders tense. He stepped closer, and she looked up at him.

"Why don't you just admit it," he said quietly.

"Admit what?"

"That you think I'm less of a person because I've got money."

"I don't think that at all. What bothers me is *how* you get your money. And how you choose to spend it."

"How could you possibly know how I spend it?"

"Come on," she said. "That car is only the tip of the iceberg. I've read about you. I've seen pictures."

"Pictures are only pictures."

She looked away. "Like I said, none of my business."

"I want to know why you think I'm so superficial."

"Why do you care?"

Now, that was an excellent question. Maybe the best one she'd asked all day. He had no idea why he cared. He'd never cared before. And he was the one who was pushing here, not the other way around. Still, he couldn't seem to let well enough alone.

"Why do you think I'm superficial, Stella?"

She fixed him with a cool gaze. "You're right. I don't know for sure how you live your life, but I can guess well enough. You've been blessed with money. I know you probably work hard for it, but you've also got a lot of people working underneath you to thank for your success, too. How much do you do for your community? Or for the people who helped you get where you are?"

It was an honest question. And one that made his face heat. The last thing he needed was Stella Clarke knowing she'd burrowed her way underneath his skin. But truth be told, she'd probably figured that out days ago.

"What?" he said, with more than a little defensiveness in his voice. "You mean, like give to charity? I do that."

That was true. It was a good tax write-off.

"Giving to charity is a great start," she said. "But there's so much more you could do, Ian. Personally."

Jill had told him the same thing once. One of the company's accountants had started a GoFundMe for his father who was in the hospital at the time. Ian had given to it, of course, but not until Jill had stood in his office with an incredulous look on her face. Since then, he usually gave something at Christmas, but let Jill decide where it was going. It was enough to ease his conscience, and that was the main objective. The fact was, when he'd left Christmas Bay, he'd also left a life of poverty and suffering behind. He simply hadn't wanted to be reminded of it, so his empathy had taken a hit over the years.

He stared down at Stella. He couldn't even fire back with a healthy, *Oh, yeah? And what are you doing to help people?* Because what she was doing was obvious. She'd come home to be with Frances, to work in the shop and help her navigate her Alzheimer's. It was a lot to commit to, but she'd committed entirely.

"So sorry that took forever!" Marley said, coming out of the back room. "She didn't want to go down right away, but I think she's finally asleep. Way past her nap time."

When she saw Ian and Stella standing so close to each other, probably looking like they were right in the middle of an argument, she frowned.

"Is everything okay?"

"Fine," Stella said. "Just…getting to know each other again."

Ian leaned away and took the club soda from Marley with a smile. "Do you have a restroom?"

"In the back to your right. But you might have to tiptoe."

"I'll be quiet. Promise."

Right then, the candy shop door opened with a tinkle of the bell, and a family with two little kids walked in. Stella welcomed them, and Marley stepped behind the counter to fiddle with the ancient cash register.

Ian made his way into the back room, careful not to wake the baby. He'd been saved by the bell. Literally. Or saved by the soda water. If he'd had to stand there another thirty seconds, he might've had to respond to the last thing Stella had said. *There's so much more you could do...*

That may be true. But he'd never been that kind of man.

Which was only going to make it harder to convince her otherwise.

Chapter Seven

Stella looked out the window at Mario's, her very favorite pizza place in the world. It had been her favorite as a kid, too, when Frances would bring her foster kids here on Friday nights, handing them a fistful of quarters and letting them play Pac-Man until their order was up.

She leaned back in one of the worn booths now, the smell of warm bread and cheese filling her senses. Only a couple more weeks until Christmas Eve and the Flotilla of Lights, the most beautiful night of the year as far as she was concerned. Tourists flocked to the bay to watch the fishing boats, strung with colorful lanterns and looking like ghostly apparitions in the fog. It was how the little town on the coast had gotten its name when the pioneers had settled here. A name befitting the Christmas lights.

Christmas… Stella bit the inside of her cheek. It would be here before she knew it, and then what? Would she have a better handle on Ian at that point? Or would she still be waffling, like she was today, balancing somewhere between not trusting him and warming to his smile, to his eyes, which seemed to change color with the light outside.

Marley walked across the room, carrying two glasses of wine. She'd left the baby with Owen tonight, who was going to introduce her to *The Little Mermaid.* Never mind that she couldn't even sit up yet. Stella suspected that he just wanted an excuse to watch it himself, since he was an overgrown kid at heart.

But he was also a wonderful dad, and he was so good to Marley, always encouraging her to do things for herself and to spend time with friends and family. Especially with Frances, knowing that someday these precious moments would fade in her foster mother's memory.

Marley definitely had a good one in Owen Taylor, and sometimes Stella found herself wondering about her own future, and if she'd eventually have someone as special to spend it with. She never used to be bothered by those kinds of thoughts, but for some reason, over the last few days, she kept coming back to them again and again. She supposed it was because of Ian and trying to figure out if he was as happy as he said he was. If he really was planning on settling down someday.

She frowned as Marley set their glasses on the table and slid into the booth opposite her. There was always the ever-present possibility he was lying about that, which was exactly why she was going to keep digging. This had started out as Frances's experiment, but it was turning into an Ian-themed mystery that Stella was determined to solve.

"What are you thinking?" Marley asked, picking up her wine and taking a sip. "You seem far away."

Stella ran her fingertip around the rim of her glass. "I don't know. About today, I guess."

"Today?"

"At the shop. With Ian."

Marley leaned back, a knowing expression on her face. "Ahh."

"What?"

"Nothing. It's just that I'm not surprised you're thinking about him."

"Well, I'm supposed to be. For Frances."

"Yeah, I know this was her idea, but now that I've seen you two together…"

Stella stiffened.

"I'm not gonna lie," Marley said. "There's some chemistry there."

"That's exactly what he said. But there's not, believe me."

"I know what I saw."

"You saw two people who don't like each other having words."

"I saw two people having words," Marley said. "The rest is up for debate."

"No way."

Marley shrugged. "I'm just saying, there's chemistry. And you denying it all day long isn't going to make it less true."

Stella finally took a sip of wine. Then she put her glass down and licked the tanginess from her lips. "I really don't know what you're talking about, Marls," she said, hoping she sounded appropriately indignant. "I'm just getting to know him again, that's all. And I'm still seeing plenty of evidence of jackassery."

"People change," Marley said.

"Now you sound like Frances."

"Well, they do. And I know it's not a popular opinion, but I always kind of liked him."

Stella stared at her.

"I know, I know," Marley said. "I never liked his *attitude* back then. But sometimes he'd let his guard down, and he could actually be kind of sweet."

"Are we talking about the same Ian?"

"I know you have to remember, too. I think you're just so dead set on not forgiving him that maybe you're refusing to admit it."

Marley was right, as usual. Stella did remember. She remembered a lot of things, actually. But she'd gotten very good at burying them because she was mad at him, and anger was more comfortable for her than the memories of his laugh, or his smile, or how they'd talked about their past once, making her feel like he understood her better than other kids had. Even though she'd never let him know that, of course. Stella had never allowed herself to be that vulnerable with anyone.

"It's not that I can't forgive him for how he could be," she said, and meant it. "It's that I know what he's up to *now*. That's what I can't forgive."

"And now that you've spent a few days with him, you still think he's up to no good?"

Stella cupped her wineglass in both hands and took a breath, ready to give her foster sister a definitive *yes*. But the strange thing was, she couldn't quite utter the word. Instead, she closed her mouth again and frowned.

"Uh-oh," Marley said. "It looks like you might be having second thoughts?"

"Not seconds thoughts exactly...but..."

"But, what?"

"I don't know. I think he might be sucking me in along with everyone else."

Marley laughed. "Welcome to the dark side."

"What happens if I can't stay objective because of his stupid charm? Then what?"

"Then we reevaluate. But I don't think we have to worry about you declaring your love just yet."

"No," Stella said. "We don't have to worry about that."

"But, can I say one thing?"

"Shoot."

"The man is gorgeous."

Stella did have to agree with that. It was impossible not to. Ian was movie-star handsome, something that was getting harder and harder to ignore. And the way he looked at her sometimes…like he could see right past her walls, straight to her heart. She was beginning to have a hard time reconciling that man with the man she thought she knew. A snake in the grass. A spider, trying to lure her into its web.

"Yes," she said. "He is."

"But it's not his looks that have you turned upside down. I know you, Stella. I think you see something redeeming in this guy. Maybe he's being honest with us. Maybe he's telling the truth about why he wants to buy Frances's house. I'm not saying I know exactly what's going on with him, but there's something more than meets the eye."

Stella gave her foster sister a small smile. "That's what I'm worried about."

Marley took a sip of her wine, watchful over the rim of her glass. "So, what now?" she asked, putting it down again.

"Now, I take him to Gracie's Christmas pageant. Maybe he'll drop some clues, or mess up somewhere. Enough for me to be able to feel one way or the other about him. And then I'll at least be able to sleep at night."

"Amen to that."

"I think Frances is planning on inviting him to coffee tomorrow," Stella said. "We'll see how that goes."

"I think out of all of us, she's the one we should worry about the most. Speaking of succumbing to his charms."

It was true. Frances was shrewd, but she also had romantic notions about Ian. She wanted to believe in him.

Stella looked over at the little tabletop Christmas tree on the pickup counter. Its plastic needles were so faded, it looked more lime green than anything, and half its lights were out. But the ones that still worked sparkled gamely through the dim lighting of the restaurant. A cheerful reminder that the holidays were almost here, and that this was the season to believe. Even if it was hard. Even if all your instincts said otherwise.

If only, she thought.

Ian sat on the couch in the living room of the old Victorian house, a fire crackling in the hearth next to him. The tangy, wood-smoke smell filled his senses, as a light rain tapped against the windows. The cat, Beauregard, had spotted him from the kitchen and immediately made a beeline for his ankles.

Ian tried scooting him away with the toe of his shoe, but just like last time, this had no effect.

"Oh, is he bothering you?" Frances asked, setting the coffee down on the end table next to a plate of sugar cookies. Christmas themed, of course. "He does seem to love you."

The cat blinked up at Ian, his yellow eyes narrowing. *I'm being judged*, Ian thought. *And it's not going well.*

"Are you sure about that?" he asked, trying not to rub his itchy eyes.

"Definitely. He doesn't do this with everyone."

Ian looked over at Frances, who had sat on the love seat opposite him. The room was warm and cozy and reminded him of a Christmas card, with the tree sparkling in the window and the cat plopped at his feet. It was so idyllic that, for a second, he wondered what the hell he was doing here. He didn't fit. He wasn't part of her family, or even a long-lost friend.

Yet, here he was. Being welcomed like someone who did fit. Like someone who mattered to her, and not in a *he's interested in my house* kind of way. He had a feeling this had nothing to do with the house at all.

He watched her take a sip of her coffee and then set it down on the end table. She stared into the fire for a long moment, lost in her thoughts.

"So, why am I here, Frances?" he asked, his voice making her startle.

She laughed. "I'd almost forgotten you were sitting there."

"I noticed."

"I was just thinking."

"About?"

"About my husband, Bud. You never got to meet him. He was a wonderful man. He loved this place."

Ian glanced over at the mantel where a framed black-and-white picture sat. It was of a young Frances, pretty and fresh-faced, standing next to a young man in bell bottoms. He had his arm around her trim waist, and she was smiling up at him adoringly. This was Bud, the love of her life. Ian had known that, even as a surly teenager. Some things didn't need an explanation.

"You two must've been very happy here," he said.

"We were. Very happy. He wanted to fill this place up with our kids." Her eyes grew misty, and she looked back over at the fire.

But they'd filled it up with foster kids instead. Kids who needed a home the most.

"He loved every single child who came to us, as if they were our own," she said. "Every single one."

Ian couldn't imagine a heart big enough for that. He didn't know if his was even capable of stretching that far. Or thawing that much. But it was a nice thought. A thought that made him sit back against the couch cushions and take a sip of his coffee, allowing himself to enjoy the moment with this nice woman who had some nice memories to share. Ian was seriously short on decent memories of his own. At least where his childhood was concerned. What would it hurt to enjoy someone else's?

"I wish I could've met him," he said. And found that he meant it.

"Oh, honey. You would've loved him. And he would've loved you, too."

"I'm not so sure about that."

"Why? Because you didn't want to be here?" She winked at him. "You were never as bad as you thought you were, Ian. You were a good boy who got dealt some bad cards, that's all. I wish you'd learn to forgive yourself."

There was a funny feeling in the back of his throat. A tickle that he immediately swallowed back down again. He'd never blamed himself for anything. He hadn't. And if he'd felt bad for how things had gone down with Frances, and for never contacting his aunt again? It was misplaced. He had nothing to feel bad for.

Except, deep down, he knew that was a bunch of crap. If he was being truthful for once, he knew he might have some things to feel bad for. Just maybe. Just maybe people had given him chance after chance, and he'd dumped on them. And that had nothing to do with how his parents had treated him, nothing to do with the damage that they'd done in his formative years. It had everything to do with

Ian, and how he was making a conscious effort, even now, to dump on people.

He cleared his throat. This house was a business deal. Nothing more, nothing less. He would give Frances every penny that it was worth, and probably more. He'd make sure she was taken care of financially. That's what he could do for her. That's all he knew how to do. At least, that's what he kept telling himself as Beauregard rubbed his little head against his pantleg again, and the fire popped and hissed in the hearth.

"What happened to him?" Ian asked, wanting to steer the subject away from himself, which seemed like a safer place to be.

"He had a heart attack," Frances said. "He passed on Christmas Eve."

Ian's pulse slowed. *Christmas Eve…*

"I'm sorry…what?"

Frances stared into the fire. "It was a long time ago. Before you or the girls came to me. But it's still hard to talk about. It's still hard to get through the holidays, even now. It's why I go so overboard on the sweaters and the earrings…" She gave him a small smile. "It's my way of keeping the joy alive, when for a lot of years, I felt like it had passed with Bud."

"I'm sorry," he said quietly. "I'm very sorry that happened to him. And to you."

"Life isn't easy. But I've got so many wonderful memories. He lives on in that way. And his legacy, of course, is you kids. He may not have met you all, but it was because of him that I kept fostering all those years. It's what he wanted. What we wanted, together."

Ian watched her. If she was as shifty as he was, it would be an Oscar-worthy performance. One that had just about choked him up. If she was the type of person to manipulate the situation, or other people around her, it would've been a moment for the books. Maybe one meant to make him come clean once and for all.

But as silence settled over the old house, the grandfather clock ticking from across the room, he knew she was simply a genuine person who'd invited him into her home and asked him to stay awhile. It was no wonder why Stella was so protective of Frances. She was a mother figure to the motherless. She gave hope to the hopeless.

Even so, even knowing this in his bones, Ian still wondered *why* she'd asked him here today. It was still hard to believe that she cared enough about him to want to have coffee, with no ulterior motives.

Taking a deep breath, he reached for his old defenses—that armor that had protected him from so much his entire life.

"So," he said evenly. Trying to remove himself from all emotion, and just focus on the matter at hand. "Why did you invite me over, Frances?"

She looked up at him, a sliver of confusion in her

blue eyes. The rain dripped down the windowpane behind her, and the wind shook the pines in the yard. It was the kind of dreary weather that could make you sad if you let it. The kind of winter day on the coast that a lot of people couldn't take. Ian could remember his mother staring out the window on days like this, lost to the world. Lost to those around her. He'd felt so alone then. Like he'd never be happy again. And of course, he hadn't been for a very long time.

"I'm sorry?" Frances asked.

"I'm still wondering why you invited me…"

"You know," she said, shaking her head. "I can't remember, honey. How do you like that? I can't remember at all."

Stella looked at her watch as the salty wind snatched at her jacket, whipping the collar up around her neck. People were filing into the elementary school doors behind her—parents, siblings, family friends. The annual Christmas Bay Elementary Holiday Pageant was a well-known event, near and far. A few years ago, it had to be moved from the auditorium to the gym to accommodate more people. This year they were doing *The Best Christmas Pageant Ever*, a fan favorite. Gracie was playing the part of Imogene Herdman, and was so nervous that Kyla said she hadn't slept a wink last night. Stage fright. Stella couldn't blame her—this was a pretty big *dill*, as Frances would say.

Stella craned her neck toward the parking lot,

looking for Ian's Porsche. He'd texted to say he was finishing up some work at the motel, and he'd meet her there. For some reason that she couldn't explain, seeing him tonight felt less like an obligation, or a mystery that needed solving, and more like a… What exactly?

She licked her lips, watching the road expectantly. There was no denying the tightness in her lower belly, the butterflies that were bumping around against her rib cage. She kept telling herself that it was because Christmas was getting closer, and pretty soon this experiment would be coming to an end. She'd need to tell Frances what she really thought of Ian. And as certain as she'd been in the beginning, she had to admit that she didn't know what she really thought of him yet. Not really. The more she got to know him, the more it felt like there was something worth getting to know. And Stella had no idea what to do with that feeling.

So, she stood on the sidewalk now, watching people walk past in their festive clothing, and tried pushing it down again. Deep down where it belonged. She had no business feeling anything for Ian, other than a little curiosity, maybe. She didn't trust him, and he wasn't her type. So, yeah. No business at all.

Across the parking lot, the silver Porsche finally made its appearance, and she raised her hand to wave as it pulled into a parking spot. Which was silly, really. He'd clearly be able to spot her waiting out front.

Still, though, when Ian climbed out of the car and waved back with that heart-stopping smile of his, she couldn't help but wonder what she was doing here. Was it to help Frances? Or were there beginning to be other reasons, too? Reasons that she couldn't understand, as hard as she'd been trying.

He crossed the parking lot and stepped up on the sidewalk, where she could immediately smell his aftershave on the breeze. He was freshly showered, his dark hair curling damply at the nape of his neck. He was wearing a pair of slacks and a winter jacket, and didn't look remotely like the high-powered real estate investor that he was. Instead, he looked like every dad here, something that made Stella's stomach tighten even more.

"I brought something for you," he said, his blue eyes sparkling in the fading evening light. Both his hands were tucked behind his back.

She stood there for a second, confused. "Something for me…"

"It's nothing big. But I saw it at the pharmacy when I went for some Tylenol and thought of you. Pick a hand."

She felt a slow smile stretch across her lips. This was something he used to do when they'd lived together at Frances's house. On those rare occasions when he would smile and be playful with his foster sisters. Stella remembered it so well, because it had charmed her, even back then.

"Ian..." she said.

"Pick a hand."

"Okay. That one."

"Nope. Pick again."

She had to work not to laugh. "That one," she said, pointing to his other hand.

He brought his fist out from behind his back and opened it. There, in his palm, was a tiny Elvis key chain. The little king was wearing a Hawaiian shirt and a lei. It was so Stella. So innately something that she would buy for herself that she had to stare at it for a minute.

"There were a bunch of them," Ian said. "They're all movie themed, I think. Anyway... I thought you'd like it. You can put it with all your Graceland memorabilia, or whatever else you've got."

He smiled down at her, and she didn't know what to say. Stella *always* had something to say. It was a blessing and a curse, Frances used to tell her. Her ability to fill a silent void with something funny, or sassy, or just plain informative. She could always put people at ease that way. And put herself at ease, too.

But for some reason, right then, standing on the blustery sidewalk with this man holding out the tiny Elvis key chain to her, she was at a complete loss for words.

His smile faded. "Are you alright?"

She nodded, and swallowed the achy feeling in

her throat. It was such a small thing, but it was so sweet of him to think of her like that.

"It's just nice of you," she said. "I really love Elvis."

"I can see that." His voice had turned soft, tender. It stroked something inside her, something that had been dormant for a long, long time. Other than her foster family, and a handful of close friends over the years, Stella wasn't in the habit of letting people in. At least not until they'd proven themselves, and most of the time, that took a while. Sometimes it took years, and quite frankly, most people didn't want to hang around that long.

But there was something about Ian that made her want to open the door for him. Just a crack. Just to see what he would do. And that was dangerous, because that's exactly how you got hurt. Stella knew from experience. She knew from her own hurt, her own trauma.

Yet, as she reached for the key chain and her fingers brushed his, she couldn't deny that's what was happening here, even on the smallest scale. By accepting this gift, and by accepting the feelings that were bubbling inside her heart, she was pushing that door open a little. She was inviting him inside.

"I can't take all the credit," he said. "I saw Frances yesterday, and we talked about you. She reminded me how much you love Elvis. So, when I saw this, I knew you had to have it. It was kismet."

She smiled, tucking the key chain into her pocket.

"Well, thank you. She told me you were meeting her for coffee. How was it?"

"It was good." An expression came over his face that she hadn't seen before. He looked especially far away. Like he was thinking deeply about something. Or feeling deeply about something.

"What else did you talk about?" she asked. "The house?"

"We talked about the house. But we also talked about Bud. I'd always wondered about him."

Stella nodded. "You know, she doesn't mention him very often. It's too painful. She must've felt comfortable opening up to you."

He was quiet at that, and she wondered how comfortable *he'd* been with it. She remembered him sitting on the wicker furniture in the sunroom looking stiff and disconnected, the day Frances had hatched this plan.

Something had definitely shifted in him over the last few days, and she was able to see it. Frances had probably been able to see it, too.

The question now was, what was that shift, and what did it mean? It could be something as simple as a change in his business approach. Or it could be something deeper, more meaningful. But how would she know for sure?

"Gracie was getting worried you weren't going to make it."

They both turned at the sound of the voice behind

them, and saw Ben standing there holding Gracie's hand. The little girl beamed up at Stella, and then let her curious gaze settle on Ian.

"Hey!" Stella said, bending down to give her a hug. Straightening again, she touched Ian's arm. "Ian, this is Ben Martinez, Christmas Bay's chief of police. Ben, this is Ian Steele."

The two men shook hands.

"Nice to meet you," Ben said.

"You too, Chief."

"And *this* little munchkin is Gracie," Stella said. "The star of tonight's show."

Ian gave her a dramatic bow. "I've never met a celebrity before. I'm pleased to meet you."

Gracie giggled, clearly charmed by this. "I'm pleased to meet you, too," she said, offering him a dainty hand.

"Don't you have to be getting ready?" Stella asked Ben. "I hope we didn't keep you."

"She wanted to wait for the entire family before going backstage. We're still pretty early, so it's fine. Whatever we can do to keep the nerves at bay."

Gracie stared up at Ian. "Are you the man Aunt Stella keeps talking about?"

Stella felt her cheeks burn, despite the chilly wind. She really didn't want Ian to know she'd been talking about him at all, but she should've anticipated this. Kids repeated *everything*.

"That would be me," he said. "I think your aunt Stella might be taken with me."

Gracie frowned. "Are you, Aunt Stella?"

"Am I…"

"Are you taking him somewhere?"

Gracie looked thoroughly confused. Ben was biting his lip, she could tell. Probably to keep from smiling. And Ian was watching her, looking pleased with himself. He always seemed pleased with himself when he'd managed to fluster her.

"No, honey," she said. "I'm not taking him anywhere."

"Then what does 'taken with' mean?"

"It means he thinks I like him."

"Do you like him?"

"They're friends, sweetie," Ben said. "She likes him as a friend."

Gracie was undeterred. "You don't like him as a boyfriend?"

Ian put his hand over his mouth and cleared his throat.

Ben gave Stella an apologetic look. "Gracie…"

"Daddy, are we going to the Christmas parade?"

Gracie looked up at her dad, bounced on her toes a few times, and just like that, the subject was changed. Stella could've cried with relief. Just like the pageant, the Christmas parade was a big deal, so it was no wonder it was on Gracie's mind. Every year half the town would brave the cold to come out and see the floats, the high school band and the rest of the entries make their way down Main Street to end up at Sandpiper Park where the city Christmas tree was.

"Honey, I have to be on duty that night. Remember I told you that Heidi is out on maternity leave?"

Gracie nodded slowly. "Her baby came out…"

"That's right, her baby came out, and she's staying home with him, and I'm short-staffed. I don't have enough officers to work the parade, which means I need to do it."

Gracie's brows knitted together. "Can Kyla take me?"

"She's going to be in the parade with her history club. They built a pirate ship float, and they need all hands on deck. *Arrgh.*" Ben winked at his own dad joke, but Gracie clearly wasn't impressed. She continued staring up at him dryly. Almost comically.

"Well, look who it is!" Frances said, appearing out of nowhere to step up on the sidewalk next to them. "Imogene Herdman in the flesh!"

The Christmas parade momentarily forgotten, Gracie grinned at her nana, who was wearing a bright red jacket with a faux fur collar, and Christmas wreath earrings that swung cheerfully next to her face.

Stella gave her foster mother a hug. "Where's Marley and Owen?"

"They're on their way. The baby had a blowout and they forgot diapers, so they had to go back to the house." She bent down and gave Gracie's cheek a squeeze. "But they'll be here soon. They wouldn't miss it."

"And Kyla's inside saving seats for everyone," Ben said. "Are we ready?"

Gracie looked up at her dad again, her dark eyes suddenly wide. "I'm nervous."

"You're gonna do great, honey."

"What if I forget my lines?"

"You won't. You know them backward and forward."

"I only know them forward. I don't know them backward, Daddy."

"That's okay," he said without skipping a beat. "Forward is all you need to know. Let's get you backstage before Miss Robin starts to worry."

"Good luck, kiddo," Stella said. "We'll be cheering from the front row."

Ben turned and led Gracie through the front doors, as Frances hooked her arm in Ian's. He looked momentarily surprised, but then smiled down at her. It was impossible not to love Frances. Given enough time, everyone did.

"Well, lucky me," Frances said. "I've got the most handsome date tonight."

"I don't know about that."

"And doesn't Stella look beautiful?"

Ian's sexy gaze settled on her, and she immediately blushed. It felt like he might know exactly what she was thinking right then, or even worse, what she was feeling. Which was attraction, plain and simple. And there were so many things wrong with that, she didn't even know where to start.

"She does look beautiful," he said, his voice low. So low that it seemed like she was the only one meant to hear. "She's always been beautiful."

Chapter Eight

Ian pushed the gym door open for Stella, and she stepped out into the cold, starry night. The wind had blown itself out, and the mist and clouds had gone with it. The ocean waves crashed against the beach a few blocks away, a dull roar that Stella could feel in her chest.

The pageant had been a smashing success. Marley, Owen and Emily had made it by the hair on their chins—another famous one-liner of Frances's—and Gracie had almost forgotten her lines because she'd been too busy grinning and waving to her family in the front row, but it had been a fun night. Ian had sat beside Stella, clearly smitten with the little kids on the stage, which was yet another thing she'd never expected to see from him. It was nice. Actually, it was more than nice. It warmed her through.

She looked up at the winter sky, at the thousands of sparkles against the velvety blackness, and sighed. "It's so beautiful."

Ian looked up, too. He was so close that she could feel his body heat, his arm brushing up against hers. A few days ago, she would've recoiled at that. But tonight, after sitting next to him throughout Gracie's pageant, after watching him hug Frances goodbye and telling her to drive safe, Stella found herself even more drawn to him. To that incredible magnetism that she'd known would be tricky for all of them in the beginning. But she hadn't expected how it would affect her. Someone who thought herself prepared for everything and affected by little.

But here she stood, her heart pounding away, sad that the night was about to end and that she'd be saying goodbye soon. This time, for good. Christmas Eve was a little over a week away now. He'd be going back to San Francisco and would be officially making an offer on the house. And then she'd have to tell Frances if she trusted him. If she thought he was a good person. At least good enough to deserve the house, her most treasured possession.

"I hated Christmas as a kid," he said quietly, still gazing up at the stars.

She looked over at him, at his handsome profile in the dim, evening light. Most everyone had gone home by now since they'd stayed to help clean up, and the parking lot was nearly empty.

She waited, listening to the sound of the ocean, of the cars passing on the highway on the outskirts of town. Somewhere in the distance a dog barked, and then another one answered.

"It was a reminder of how screwed up my life was," Ian continued. "Of how screwed up my family was. I just wanted normal, you know? Just...*normal*."

He turned and looked down at her, and his eyes were bright. They reflected the light of the streetlamps in their pale blue pools. They shone like the stars overhead. But mostly, they looked sad. She recognized that look, because she'd seen it in her own reflection growing up. The sadness, the despair.

"I know," she said, feeling her throat tighten. "I wanted normal, too."

He nodded, watching her. How many times had she cried herself to sleep when she'd been little? Too many times to count. She remembered all the Christmases, the holidays, the birthdays that were ruined by the fighting, that more often than not ended in some kind of violence. She'd longed for peace, like her friends had. She'd longed for love and safety and happiness. And then, miraculously, she'd gotten all those things, just like she'd wished for. She'd gotten them with Frances.

It seemed like Ian might've been thinking the

same thing, because his expression relaxed. The look in his eyes warming, just a little.

"Then, when I finally got normal," he said, "I went and sabotaged it. Why did I do that? Why did I do that to myself?"

"Because you were sixteen," she said. "You were just a kid."

"You were a kid, too. And you stayed. You realized what you'd been given. Why couldn't I?"

He looked so vulnerable right then that she was having trouble not stepping closer to him. Which wasn't smart, she knew. What if she did step close, what would she do then? Wrap her arms around his waist? Look up into his eyes and ask for something that he couldn't give?

Instead, she bit her cheek until the pain brought her back to reality. "You couldn't, because you were too angry. And you had every right to be angry, Ian. We all did."

"But not at Frances."

"No, but she understood. She never held it against you."

"But you did."

"I was a kid, too."

"You're still angry, though."

"I thought I was…"

His gaze was so intense that her stomach dipped. She could feel her pulse tapping behind her ears. It was making her dizzy. She had no idea how she'd let herself spiral like this. There was no explanation, except that maybe Ian's pull was even stronger than she'd thought. She still believed he was shallow, self-ish, cunning... But maybe she didn't believe those things as strongly as before. Maybe she was start-ing to feel like she could see past the surface Ian, to the man underneath, and that was definitely mak-ing her dizzy.

"If you're not angry anymore," he said, "then what are you?"

She shook her head. "I don't know. Confused, I guess."

"About me?"

He was pinning her in place with those eyes. She couldn't have looked away if she'd tried. She'd never seen eyes as beautiful as Ian's.

"Yes," she said quietly.

"Why?"

"Because I feel like there's something between us now, and I don't know what that is. And it doesn't matter, anyway, because we're like oil and water."

He smiled at that. Stepped a little closer. She could feel the electricity pulsing between them. "You're right on one of those counts," he said.

"Oh, yeah? Which one?"

"There's definitely something between us..."

The tips of her ears began to throb.

"But we're more alike than you think, Stella."

She stared up at him. *We're more alike than you*

think… Deep down, she was actually starting to believe that.

"We both started out the same way in life," he said. "We both share that experience. Not everyone can understand it."

That was true. And something that she'd had to face over and over again, especially with her relationships as an adult. Whenever she'd meet someone who came from a stable, loving family, they immediately wanted to know all about hers. Either she found herself avoiding the subject altogether, or stretching the truth in order to make them more comfortable with her past. She didn't want anyone's pity, and because of that, she didn't open up easily. She guessed a lot of foster kids probably felt that way as they got older. It was a club that nobody wanted to belong to. But she and Ian did belong, and it bonded them, whether they liked it or not.

"And we both care about Frances," he continued. "We both want what's best for her."

"I want to believe that," she said warily. "I really, really do."

"Then believe it."

"It's not that easy."

Still, she was feeling herself soften like clay underneath his warm gaze. She'd known Ian could coax certain emotions out of people. It was his gift. With her, in the beginning, it had been anger. Hot and sparking. But tonight, it was something else. She felt it rising up inside her, something exciting and forbidden. It was the way he looked at her, like she was desirable. Like she was special to him. And she'd never felt that way before. Not like this.

"I don't think I've ever met anyone so loyal," he said. "You really would do anything for your family, wouldn't you?"

"I really would."

He put his hands in his pockets then and rocked back on his shoes. The muscles in his jaw bunched and relaxed, his black hair gleaming underneath the light from the streetlamps. He looked like Clark Kent, only without the glasses, and she was overwhelmed with the temptation to step forward and put her hands in his hair. To bring his mouth down to hers. To kiss him long and hard. She felt herself sway toward him, just a little. Licking her lips, she swallowed hard and tried to steady herself, but her heart was pounding too hard to feel steady at all.

She needed to leave *now.* She needed to go home and get a handle on whatever this was. Whatever he was doing to her. Or whatever she was letting him do to her.

"You know," she said quietly, "I should really get back. The roads are slick, and Frances will start to worry."

He nodded, but didn't take his eyes off her. "Of course."

She waited another few seconds, feeling like there

was more to say, but of course, there wasn't. She'd just been tempted to kiss him, and that said it all.

"Okay, then," she said. "Good night."

"Good night, Stella."

Without another look, she forced herself to turn and walk away. And felt him watching her until she climbed into her Jeep and turned the key in the ignition.

As she pulled out of the parking lot and onto the dark, rain soaked road, she couldn't help but wonder what would've happened if she'd stayed.

Ian threw his keys on the motel room dresser and took off his jacket. He couldn't see the ocean outside the window in the inky darkness, but he could hear the now familiar sound of the waves crashing on the beach. So familiar that it was almost comforting, like a lullaby in those early morning hours, when he'd finally put his laptop away and turn off the light.

He'd gotten into the habit of lying on his back with his head in the crook of his arm, and listening to the ocean, churning and restless in the distance. That's how he'd always thought of himself. Restless. Never wanting to slow down, never wanting to stay in one place too long. That's why San Francisco suited him so well—whenever he thought about slowing down, even a little, another deal popped up, another opportunity that needed chasing down.

But now that he was back here, back in Christmas

Bay, the thought of easing his foot off the gas was beginning to tempt him at unexpected moments. Like tonight, when he'd stood there looking down at Stella in the cold, silver clouds puffing from her mouth.

Where was this coming from?

Rolling up the sleeves of his dress shirt, he walked over to the darkened window and looked up at the stars overhead. He couldn't get used to how many of them there were. They looked like spilled table salt, scattered over the heavens. They were beautiful. Just another thing he'd never taken the time to appreciate before.

He crossed his arms over his chest, shifting his gaze to his reflection in the glass. It was probably just his imagination, but he felt like he looked different. Maybe it was his hair, grown slightly longer since he'd been here. He didn't trust anyone in Christmas Bay to give him a trim. Or maybe it was the stubble. He hadn't shaved this morning and had been thinking of letting it go for a few days. He'd probably look like a lumberjack by the time Christmas rolled around. But when in Rome, right?

Even as he thought it, though, he knew those things weren't really why he looked different. It was because he felt different. And there was an expression in his eyes that brought that realization home. Something that unsettled him, and made him turn away from his reflection.

He pulled his cell phone from his pocket and tapped

the screen to see a list of text messages from the office. It was a welcome distraction. For the last half hour, all he'd been able to think about was Stella. Her hair, her skin, her eyes, which were wide and dark and lovely. He'd been about to lean down and kiss her tonight. He'd actually had to clench his fists at his sides when she'd gazed up at him and licked her lips. His self-control had been stretched to the limit, making him wonder if he had the strength to let her walk away from him. And then, miraculously, he had. He'd thought about it all the way back to the motel, his heart thumping in his chest. He'd been about to kiss her, and then what? What the hell would he have done after that?

He knew what he would've done. He would've used that kiss to his advantage. He would've used it to get what he wanted, and what he wanted was the house. The thought, for the first time ever, made him slightly sick to his stomach.

Sitting heavily on the bed, he narrowed his eyes at his phone. One of the texts was from Carter. He clicked on it and read it with an undeniable tightening in his gut.

What gives? I need an update on this property. Is it happening? Time frame? Call me tomorrow. I've got back-to-back meetings until three, but will be free after!

He ran a hand through his hair and set the phone on the nightstand, not bothering to read the other texts.

What he needed to do, ASAP, was remember why he'd come up here in the first place. Sure, he'd wanted to mess with Stella a little. But it wasn't because of her that he'd come. It was because of the property.

He hated how it felt like he was trying to convince himself of that now.

Leaning back against the headboard, he closed his eyes and listened to the sound of the crashing waves. Stella had booked a deep-sea fishing trip with her and Owen for tomorrow afternoon. She was going all out with this showing-him-around thing. She was probably hoping he'd fall overboard or something.

He shifted on the bed and took a deep breath, his eyes still closed. The truth was, he really wasn't sure what Stella was hoping for. The look in her eyes tonight made him think she might be a little disappointed if he fell overboard. Just a little.

It's the property, he repeated silently to himself. *Only the property...*

Stella stepped onto the deck of the fishing boat, the *Agatha Marie*, which was rocking heavily against the dock. Owen grabbed her hand to steady her. Even standing still, it was hard to stand still.

Ian stepped down beside them, looking quiet, his skin pale against his black rain jacket. She'd wanted him to feel uncomfortable, out of place, when she'd made the reservation, but she was starting to feel bad for making him do this. He hadn't said anything about being prone to seasickness, but he was so stubborn, she wouldn't be surprised if he'd just left that out. This was a game, after all, and the best opponent was going to win.

The chilly wind whipped her hair against her neck, and she pulled her knit cap farther down over her ears.

Owen grinned and slapped Ian on the back. "You sure you want to go out today, man? We don't have to. They give rain checks if the wind picks up, and I want you to have a good time."

Ian's jaw muscles bunched, but he smiled gamely at Owen. "No, it's okay. We should go. Christmas is almost here, and then it'll be too late."

Maybe he meant there wouldn't be any more charters over the holidays. But Stella thought he was probably talking about the countdown to their Christmas deadline. When she would have to decide if he was trustworthy or not.

The thought of it made her stomach turn. Or maybe that was the fishy smell coming from the back of the boat.

Owen grinned. He was a former star pitcher, now the head coach for the Christmas Bay Tiger Sharks, but he didn't look like either of those things. He looked like a surfer with his blond, windblown hair and tan skin. He looked right at home on the *Agatha Marie*, with his jacket pulled high around his neck, which was probably because he had a small boat himself. He was used to the water, and he was used to being out in the weather.

Ian, probably not so much.

Stella frowned, watching the other man hold on to the railing as the boat pitched back and forth.

"You folks ready to catch some fish?" the guide asked behind them.

They all nodded, trying to brace themselves against the swaying.

"It's choppy this afternoon," he continued. "Any choppier and we wouldn't go out. But it should be fine once we get past the swells. If you brought any Dramamine, I'd take it now."

She looked dubiously at Ian, who'd turned slightly green. She stepped forward and grabbed his hand. It was warm, despite how pale he looked. She squeezed his fingers—long, blocky, strong. She wondered if she would've ever had the courage to touch him under any other circumstance.

"Ian," she said. "You don't have to do this."

His blue gaze settled on her. "Why wouldn't I?"

"Because you think you have something to prove. And to be completely honest... I was being kind of mean and thought this might happen. A lot of people get seasick deep-sea fishing."

"Oh." He smiled, but it was wobbly. "Now we're getting down to it."

She felt her cheeks heat, despite the chilly wind blowing against them. Then she realized she was still holding his hand and tried pulling it away, but he squeezed gently before she could.

"I'll be fine," he said. "And you're right. I do have something to prove."

"Folks," the guide said. "There are life jackets in the bin up front. We need you to pick one out, and we'll come by and make sure they're secured properly. We'll be pushing off the dock in just a few minutes. There's seating inside, which we recommend, to keep you dry from the spray in the harbor."

There was a newlywed couple on the boat, laughing and cuddling each other, and a father and son digging through the life jackets. All in all, their small group seemed excited for the adventure, even if it was so cold, Stella was having a hard time keeping her teeth from clicking together.

Owen tossed her a life jacket. "Here you go. Don't smell it, whatever you do."

"I'll try not to."

Ian looked at his watch. "So, how long do you think we'll be out? I have to call into the office around three."

"We should be back before that," Owen said. "Honestly, I think once we get out there, it'll be too choppy to stay. These guys are die-hard, but they can't have their customers hurling overboard the entire time, either."

At that, Ian swallowed visibly.

Stella resisted the urge to ask again if he was okay.

He'd made up his mind, she could tell. But at this point, she couldn't understand why. Was he really trying to win her over because of the house? Or was it something else now? The warmth in his hands, in his eyes, made her think it might be something else.

But of course, that was silly. She was *wanting* it to be something else, because something had happened to her last night in the parking lot of the elementary school. She'd let herself be drawn in, just like she'd been afraid of. It had happened. With the little Elvis key chain, and the way Ian had looked at her under those streetlamps. She'd been pulled in by his incredible magnetism, and now she was standing here, fiddling with the clips on her life jacket, imagining that he was actually wanting to stay for reasons other than his own gain.

He reached out to help her with the clip, probably noticing that her hands were shaking.

"Here," he said. "Let me get that."

She gazed up at him. If she wasn't careful, she really was going to fall, hook, line and sinker, and then what?

She couldn't even fathom.

Ian looked at his watch—it wasn't even two yet, and the *Agatha Marie* was on her way back to the dock. *Thank God.* The fishing trip had been short-lived. Just like Owen had predicted, it had been too choppy to stay.

Stella sat beside him now, watching the bay outside the foggy window. Ironically, the water was much calmer now, the wind having died down almost as soon as they'd turned around. The poor guides had to have loved that. Not great for business, even if it wasn't anything they could control.

Owen was at the front of the boat, chatting amiably with the father and son duo, the latter of which was in absolute awe. Apparently, he was a huge Tiger Sharks fan, and an even bigger Owen Taylor fan. Ian smiled. It had been fun to watch the boy, who was probably in sixth or seventh grade, ask excited questions about minor-league baseball. His dad had to put a steadying hand on his shoulder at one point, saying, "Son, take a breath."

Owen seemed to be in his element. He'd promised to send them tickets to the first home game in the spring—even bringing his phone out to get their address before he forgot.

Ian liked him, and he didn't usually warm up to people this fast. He faked it all the time, but this was different. In fact, most of the people Stella had introduced him to over the last week—from Henry at the diner, to her foster sisters' significant others, to her favorite locals at the candy shop, he'd liked. Which surprised the hell out of him, quite frankly. He was even starting to develop a soft spot for Loretta, the nosy front desk lady, which told him about all he needed to know—he was letting this place get to him.

"You're awfully quiet," Stella said, turning to him. "You're not still feeling sick, are you?"

"I never felt that sick."

She smiled.

"Okay. Maybe I felt a *little* sick."

"Well, that's what your general pallor would suggest."

"I can't believe you were hoping I'd get sick."

"I wasn't *hoping*."

"But you weren't going to feel bad if I did."

"No, I was already starting to feel bad."

"Well, then. I've got you right where I want you."

He'd been smiling when he said it, looking down into her pretty face. Apparently, it didn't matter if Stella's hair was hopelessly windblown and she didn't have a stitch of makeup on. She was absolutely beautiful.

He took a deep breath, trying to concentrate on the smell of the salty sea air instead of her scent, which reminded him of wildflowers. He really didn't know how he'd gotten to this place, where breathing her in made his heart beat faster. Where seeing her every day was becoming something he looked forward to. Where falling for her, *really* falling for her, was becoming more of a stark reality than an abstract thought.

This realization was beginning to have him unsettled. But then again, a lot of things were beginning to have him unsettled. The ever-present feeling of guilt, for one. The genuine affection he was starting to have for Frances, for another. Not to mention, Christmas Bay. He hated this place. Or, at least he'd thought he hated it. Turns out his feelings for his hometown were never that easy, never that cut-and-dried. They were layered and intricate.

Ian had never been a fan of layered and intricate. Because layers needed peeling back. Intricacy needed taking a closer look. They needed patience and care, and he wasn't interested in either of those things. He'd never been before, anyway. What were the odds that he'd change now?

"Can I ask you a question?" Stella said, her thigh warm and soft against his. She was wearing jeans today, nothing special, but everything she wore tended to turn him on. She was a very sexy woman. She was beautiful, but it was more than that. Stella was also smart and capable. She was comfortable in her own skin, which made her extremely alluring. He wondered if anyone had ever told her that before. It was a line he'd have no problem spouting off to any other woman, but for some reason, the thought of saying it to Stella filled him with a dangerous kind of heat.

"Sure," he said. "Ask away."

"If you could live anywhere in the world, where would it be?"

He watched her, intrigued by this. Because the answer he'd normally give—overseas, of course!—

didn't spring to mind right away. In fact, the answer that was teetering on his lips was something very different. For him, at least.

"Why do you ask?" he said.

"I'm still trying to get to the bottom of you, Ian."

"To the bottom of me, or the bottom of my intentions?"

"Both."

"Ah. Well, then. We could be here all day."

"You're that deep?"

"I'm that deep."

She smiled, but kept her gaze on him. The boat rocked, the sound of its engine a low roar in his ears. But he barely noticed. Stella was suddenly all he cared about. Not the house, not the property, not the deal he was closing in on. Right that minute, none of that mattered in the least. What mattered was this woman whom he didn't want to leave this afternoon. He wanted to spend the rest of the day with her. And he wanted to spend the night with her, too.

He leaned closer, until he could see the flecks of brown in her eyes. Until he could see the individual freckles scattered across her nose.

"I'm about to kiss you, Stella Clarke," he said softly, not caring that everyone else on the boat might be watching. Right now, it was just him and Stella. Maybe it had always been him and Stella. "So, if you don't want to be kissed, you'd better tell me now."

They were attracted to each other, sure. That was

obvious. But he was still half expecting her to push him away. Because he wasn't the nice guy he was pretending to be, after all.

But she didn't push him away. Instead, her soft, heart-shaped lips parted, and she whispered the sweetest two words he thought he'd ever heard.

"Kiss me," she said.

Bending close, he hovered over her mouth. Just for a few, painful seconds. Because he wanted her to want this as much as he did. He wanted her heart to be pounding away inside that lovely chest, like his was pounding now. He wanted her to reach for him, because she simply couldn't stand not to anymore.

And then, she did.

Slowly, she put her hands on either side of his face. He could feel them trembling a little, as she rubbed her thumbs along his jaw. The feel of her skin against his, the softness and warmth of her fingers, sent bolts of heat straight to his stomach. And all of a sudden, he was the one who couldn't stand it anymore.

With a low sound inside his throat, he finally pressed his lips to hers, trying to be gentle and slow. Trying to be everything he thought she'd want, because nothing else mattered.

He flicked his tongue against her full, velvety lips, and she parted her mouth with a soft sigh. She tasted like something he'd been hungry for his entire life, and his body hummed with the pleasure of just now discovering it.

Ian had kissed a lot of women. He'd romanced them, and brought them home, and tried to let them down easy if they fell in love. He, himself, never had a problem with falling in love. When you were a cold, hard bastard, sex was really the only thing you were concerned with in the end.

But right then, as the boat rocked and the wind blew, and as Stella kissed him back, he realized his world as he knew it was about to change.

Chapter Nine

Stella walked beside Ian on the dock, his hand on the small of her back as he guided her around a pile of fishing nets and sun-bleached life preservers.

"Careful," he said.

Owen hadn't waited for them. He'd seen them kiss and had given her a knowing grin from the front of the boat. When they'd docked, he'd climbed the stairs with a quick wave over his shoulder, obviously wanting to give them privacy, like they were on some kind of date or something.

And now that they *were* alone, the other passengers long since having made a beeline for the warmth of their cars in the parking lot, Stella's face still felt hot. Her heart was knocking around in her chest like it was trying to find a way out.

Ian, for his part, hadn't said much. He walked alongside her now, having taken away his hand again to bury it in his jacket pocket. She knew he had to call into the office pretty soon, so maybe he was thinking about work. Or maybe he was thinking about that kiss. About how his lips had moved so expertly over hers, and how she'd arched her back in response. She'd been lost in the moment. Not thinking, only feeling.

She looked over at him now, almost shyly. And Stella hadn't felt shy in years. This was what Ian had done to her. He'd stripped away her defenses, like bark from a sapling. Now she felt as vulnerable as she ever had.

He smiled, but seemed far away. She could only guess what he was thinking as the seagulls swooped and squabbled overhead.

After a few seconds, he cleared his throat. "So, the parade…"

She waited, confused.

"If Gracie still wants to go," Ian said, "you and I could take her…"

Stella smiled hesitantly. She wasn't sure if she was being played or not. Was this slick, calculating, real estate mogul Ian? Or was it the Ian who'd just taken her breath away on the *Agatha Marie*?

He slowed, then came to a stop and leaned against the dock railing. She slowed, too, watching him carefully.

"What?" he said.

"Nothing."

"That's not true. What is it?"

She looked past him to the bay beyond. In only a week, the biggest Christmas event of them all would be here. The Flotilla of Lights would usher in Christmas Eve, and then this contest, or whatever it was with Ian, would be over. She would know exactly why he'd come, exactly why he'd stayed. And then, her heart might end up broken. Not to mention, Frances's.

Suddenly, her racing heartbeat, flushed cheeks and feeling of vulnerability annoyed her. Where were all her defenses? It appeared that Ian had the ability to make them vanish, just like that. It was like he had a magic wand, and with one casual wave... *poof!* She was reduced to nothing more than a business deal that needed securing.

"I need to know, Ian," she said evenly. Wanting him to know she meant business, too. "What are your intentions with Frances's house?"

He looked down at her, and she could tell he hadn't been expecting this. More kissing maybe, but not this.

After a second, the corner of his mouth curved. "That's no secret," he said. "I'm going to live in it."

The expression on his face was teasing. He was trying for the banter they'd gotten so good at over the last few days. But she wasn't in the mood for it, no matter how handsome he looked standing there.

She needed him to come clean now. She couldn't wait for the Flotilla and Christmas Eve, and the sweet, hopeful look on her foster mother's face. She had to know now.

"Ian…"

He gazed down at her and then reached for her hand. He made her feel like he was leading her somewhere, but she didn't know where. All she knew was that she wanted to go. She *wanted* to trust him, and that scared her.

"I'm going to live in it, Stella," he said. "And that's the truth."

This was the second time Ian found himself in front of Weatherly Court. But this time, he'd actually stopped. He'd pulled over next to the curb, put the Porsche into neutral and taken a deep, painful breath.

He sat there now, the car's motor purring into the night air, watching as a few elderly men made their second trip around the building. They were walking at a brisk pace, arms pumping, their breath puffing from their mouths in silver clouds. They wore sweats and knitted hats, and looked to be in pretty good shape for living in a place like this. Surely, all the residents couldn't be in such good health.

His chest tightened as he thought of his aunt. Actually, he hadn't been able to stop thinking of his aunt, and that's what had him sitting here now, like some sort of weirdo stalker of senior citizens. He just hoped nobody would call the police. With his luck, Ben would show up, and then this delicate trust forming with Stella would be shattered once and for all.

Ian scrubbed his face with his hands. He was in deep now. Deeper than he'd ever planned on being. He'd had no clue when he drove up here a week ago that he'd end up feeling this way. Him, of all damn people. He didn't get sucked into cheesy family Christmas events. His heart wasn't affected by small-town hospitality, or little kid excitement at the mention of Santa. He didn't care about people from his childhood, least of all Stella Clarke.

But the problem was, all those things he'd believed about himself, about what kind of person he'd always been, were starting to be questionable. Now he needed to figure out where to go from here. What he really wanted was to feel the way he had when he'd rolled into town—confident, maybe a little arrogant, with a clear-cut mission to accomplish. Instead of the sentimental gob of mush that he was turning into.

He watched the men coming back around the building, this time waving to an elderly woman walking in the opposite direction. She waved back, smiling wide.

Ian sighed and thought of the question Stella had asked on the boat. *If you could live anywhere in the world, where would it be?* He hadn't answered her. He hadn't answered her, because he'd immediately thought of a small town, not unlike Christmas Bay. A town where he could get to know people, and they could get to know him. A place where he might actually settle down someday. Maybe even Christmas Bay itself.

But of course, he hadn't said that, because it was ridiculous. He'd been caught up in the moment, that was all. It was simply a feeling that had materialized after going to that Christmas pageant of Gracie's. After sitting in Frances's house drinking coffee, and having her look at him like she cared. After sitting next to Stella on that boat, her scent making him heady, possibly even making him lose his mind a little. It was all those things, and now he had to get right again.

If only he hadn't kissed her. If only he'd been able to resist the attraction. If only he could shake whatever this was…

But even as he thought it, he felt a funny tightening in his gut. Because he hadn't called Carter today like he'd needed to. It was the reason he'd had to get back by three from the fishing trip—he'd even told Owen and Stella that. But when he'd left her at the dock and climbed into the Porsche, he'd sat there for a long time and hadn't called. He'd told himself he'd call when he got back to the motel, but he hadn't called then, either. And when Carter had called him, he'd hit decline, texting her to say he was busy right then. But he wasn't busy. He was just thinking. Thinking, thinking, thinking.

And now, here he was. Watching the retirement home across the street, and waiting for what exactly? For his aunt to materialize out front? Maybe wearing a bedazzled Christmas sweatshirt like the ones Frances was so fond of? Or pushing a walker with a jingle bell wreath on the front?

He rubbed the stubble on his chin. So, yeah. He was in deep. The line between his original intentions and his true desires was so hazy, he couldn't even see it anymore.

He just prayed things would come back into focus before Christmas Eve. Before all those things he'd thought he'd known about himself disappeared like a boat in the mist.

Stella held Gracie's mittened hand and smiled down at her. She was so darn cute. Her purple hat, something that Frances had crocheted for her last fall, was falling down over one eye, the little white pom-pom drooping off to the side. It was hopelessly big, but maybe she'd grow into it. Her puffy pink jacket was zipped all the way to her chin, making her face look rounder than it actually was. She looked like a legitimate elf from Santa's workshop, which was perfect, since she was waiting with bated breath for the big man himself.

Ian stood on the other side of her, the chilly night

air making his nose red. But he still managed to look gorgeous in his fitted black ski jacket and jeans. Whereas Stella probably looked like she was headed to a church Christmas bazaar in her knitted hat and matching mittens. But her heart was so full, she didn't want to ruin it by mentally comparing herself to the women Ian was probably used to dating. After all, Stella *was* a Christmas bazaar kind of girl. And as he looked at her now, she could tell he liked what he saw. Or, at least, he was doing a pretty good job of pretending.

He smiled, dimples cutting deep into his scruffy cheeks. He looked so sexy with the beginnings of a beard, more comfortable and relaxed. Something had happened to him over the last week, and she could see the same changes in herself. It was some kind of metamorphosis that was making her say and do things that she wouldn't normally do. And for some reason, some of the wariness where Ian was concerned had eased tonight. Maybe it was the magic of the parade, or the joy etched on Gracie's face. Or maybe it was the kiss that was lulling her into a false sense of security. Whatever it was, Stella just felt happy.

Gracie squeezed her hand and grinned as the Elks Lodge entry passed by—about a dozen elderly men in Santa hats playing kazoos. One of them tossed a handful of candy in Gracie's direction, and it scattered at her feet.

She squealed and gathered it up, stuffing it into her pockets like a squirrel hoarding nuts for the winter.

"We should've brought a wheelbarrow," Ian said looking down at her. "Or an extra pair of pants."

Gracie giggled. Stella knew that gummy worms from Coastal Sweets were her absolute favorite, but it was obvious she was willing to make an exception tonight.

"I thought that was you!"

All three of them turned at the sound of a woman's voice behind them. It had almost been drowned out by the marching band coming around the corner. Stella could feel the drum beats reverberating in her chest.

Standing there, wearing a chic wool jacket and a matching gray beanie, was Gwen Todd, the reporter from *Coastal Monthly*. She had her camera bag slung over one shoulder.

Stella smiled at her. So did Ian, but she thought she saw a strange expression cross his face. It was really only a flicker of something that she couldn't place, and then it was gone.

"Hi, Gwen," she said, trying to push down the momentary feeling of foreboding. "Happy holidays."

"Happy holidays to you," Gwen said. "And who's this?"

Gracie grinned up at her. "I'm Gracie."

"Nice to meet you, Gracie. What a pretty name. Are you excited about Santa?"

"Yep. I'm gonna ask for a Nintendo Switch for Christmas."

Gwen's eyes widened. "Wow. Have you been a good girl all year?"

Gracie nodded, looking confident about this.

"Well, then," Gwen continued, "I'll be crossing my fingers for you."

Gracie smiled, then turned back to the parade. The band was passing in front of them now, and the music was so loud, it was hard for Stella to hear herself think.

"So, the article comes out tomorrow," Gwen said, leaning close so Ian and Stella could hear her over the brass and drums. "It was fun to work on. I hope it helps Frances sell the house."

"I'm sure it will," Ian said. But his voice sounded tight.

"Thank you for everything," Stella said. "I can't wait to read it."

Gwen looked up at Ian curiously. "I was surprised to see you here. Did you come back for a visit?"

"Not exactly. Long story."

She nodded, looking interested in that. Gwen Todd was definitely a natural journalist. She probably wanted nothing more than for Ian to explain. In detail.

"Okay, then," she said. "I need to run. Taking pictures at the park when Santa gets there. A reporter's job is never done."

Stella watched her make her way through the crowd, and then disappear behind a food truck selling funnel cakes and hot cocoa. Seeing her just now was unsettling. And it was obvious why. It brought to mind the ever-present question of what was going to happen with Frances's house. She'd managed to bury it for a few hours, but it was still there, lurking underneath the surface.

Ian watched her go, too. He was frowning now, a wrinkle between his dark brows.

"We let ourselves forget about it, didn't we?"

He glanced over at her, still frowning. Looking far away. "What?"

"Nothing," she said. But her voice was drowned out by the band.

Ian sat up in bed and stared at his phone. Then he rubbed his eyes to make sure he was reading the text message right.

Have to be in Portland to meet with a client tomorrow. Haven't been able to reach you, so I'm flying up a day early. I'll rent a car and come into Christmas Bay. I'm curious to see this property in person, anyway. See you around six!

He scraped a hand through his hair. *Carter.* This was what he got for ignoring her calls. For trying to put off the inevitable. Technically, this surprise visit shouldn't bother him. Why would it? He and Carter had looked at hundreds of properties together over the years. But this one…this one was different.

And why was that? He knew why. He was having second thoughts about buying this property. Actually, that wasn't quite true. He was having second thoughts about buying this property for the building opportunities and resale value. And that was something Carter most definitely wouldn't understand. Hell, *he* didn't even understand it.

He stared out the window where the sky was just now turning pink and orange in the east. As much as he wanted to put Carter off, he knew he was going to have to deal with her. She wasn't going away. When it came to business, she was like a bulldog—once she grabbed on, she didn't let go. He'd just have to explain that this was a delicate situation where the owner was concerned. He'd show her the property on the down-low, they'd have dinner to discuss it and that would be that. He wasn't going to mention any second thoughts he was having, because quite frankly, he'd probably come back around by the time she got here, anyway. This was just a hiccup. A temporary blip on the screen. Buying Frances's house for anything other than reselling it didn't make any sense. What was he going to do? Actually *live* there, like he was trying to get Stella to believe? A second home that he'd knock around in once or twice a year? No, thanks.

Still, there was a nagging thought that kept coming back to him again and again. Who said he had to live there? What if he bought it privately, didn't sell it and did something else with it? At least for a while. And then if he ever *wanted* to live in it, well, then...

Scowling, he shook his head, as if to rid it of the idea once and for all. What in God's name had gotten into him? *No.* No, no, no. This wasn't why he'd spent the last week of his life working this sale. He didn't want to own a house in Christmas Bay. He didn't want to live here. *Ever.*

Before he could think any more about it, he threw the covers back and stepped onto the worn carpet. He needed to go for a run. He needed to get out of this room and into the morning air, and start remembering all the reasons he'd hated this place from the beginning. And if he ran into Loretta, the front desk lady? He would not be swayed by her kindly, small-town talk, or her sweet, well-meaning compliments, or her ever-present Christmas attire. The Ian of a few weeks ago would've eaten people like Loretta for breakfast.

It was time to reconnect with that Ian, and tell this new Ian to bugger the hell off.

Stella turned the Jeep onto the bumpy dirt road that led up the hill to Frances's house. There was a hot pepperoni and mushroom pizza from Mario's on the seat next to her that smelled like heaven and was making her stomach growl. She was planning on surprising her foster mother tonight—she'd closed the shop early, and there was a new season of *The Crown* that they'd been meaning to get to for weeks now. It was a perfect night for it, foggy and cold, and Stella knew there would be a crackling fire in the fireplace, and Beauregard would be ripe for cuddling—he was always ripe for cuddling.

She was looking forward to some quality time with Frances. She knew they'd probably talk about Ian, and that was okay. She'd been trying to avoid the subject for days now, but she finally felt relaxed enough, confident enough, to go there. Frances would ask what she thought about him so far. She'd ask if she trusted him, and Stella thought the answer to that would be yes. Ian had opened up to her, and, at least during those brief moments, she thought she could see past his infamous ego, past all his defenses, to the man inside.

She squeezed the steering wheel now, thinking about that kiss. Thinking about his mouth on hers, and how he made her feel. She'd finally gotten to a place where trust was at least possible, if not a completely forgone conclusion. She was willing to give him the benefit of the doubt, and for her, that was a very big deal.

The Jeep bounced over a pothole in the road, and she slapped her hand over her phone to keep it from sliding off the pizza box. He'd texted earlier that afternoon, asking if she was going to be at the shop all day. She'd said yes, thinking she would be, but the temptation to close early and pig out had simply been too strong to resist.

As she maneuvered the Jeep around another rut in the road, the house came into view through a break in the shadowy trees. Before she could stop herself, she thought about Christmas Eve, and what Ian was going to do after the holiday. Even though she was sure he'd be going back to San Francisco—of course he would be, he lived there—she wondered how soon he'd be coming back to Christmas Bay. If she was right, like she hoped she was, and he did end up buying the house for himself, that meant he'd be back soon. What would that mean for them?

Her cheeks warmed. She was embarrassed that she'd let herself hope for more. Just because he might have future ties to this town did not mean he'd have ties to her. She and her foster sisters would move Frances out of the house and into a cozy place of her choosing, and they might not ever have reason to see Ian again. Except for around town, of course, but that was about it. Stella was a realist, and this was realistic thinking.

Even so, she was determined to be happy about the house, at least. If things happened the way she hoped they would, and the property didn't end up on the market again after Ian bought it, she'd be grateful for that part. And the feelings for him that were blossoming inside her? She'd just have to wrestle them into submission. No matter how he looked at her, or how his lips felt on hers. Ian wasn't the type to have his head turned by someone like her, at least not for long. They were too different. And she would tell herself that hourly, if that's what it took to protect her heart.

Shifting into first, she pushed the Jeep up the last bit of the hill, and then turned into Frances's drive. The gravel crunched underneath the tires as she looked over and saw a beautiful silver Porsche parked in front of the garage.

Ian. At the sight of the car, Stella's pulse thrummed at the base of her throat. What was he doing here? She quickly racked her brain, trying to remember if Frances had mentioned inviting him over. Of course, she didn't need to run her social calendar by Stella, but her foster mother usually told her everything that was going on in her life, especially if it had to do with Ian Steele.

She pulled up next to the Porsche and cut the Jeep's engine. It was starting to get dark, and the Christmas tree in the window glowed through the dusky evening light. The icicle lights hanging on the eaves of the house twinkled like stars, and sure enough, there was smoke curling from the chimney. She stepped out into the cold night air, breathing in the tangy scent of wood smoke and pine. Then she walked around to the passenger's side of her car to get the pizza.

For some reason, she felt cold fingers of apprehension tickle the back of her neck. It wasn't that Ian couldn't stop by to visit Frances if he wanted to, but what had prompted this?

She made her way to the front door, unable to stop asking herself that question. Because it was starting to occur to her that maybe that text from him earlier in the afternoon had some deeper meaning. Maybe he'd wanted to know if she was going to be away from the house for a reason…

Surely, she was just being suspicious. Still, though, as she pushed the door open and stepped inside, she didn't call out that she was home like she normally would've. She didn't call out, because she could immediately hear a hushed conversation coming from around the corner, in the breakfast nook. A conversation between Ian and a woman that wasn't Frances.

Stella looked around. Her foster mother was nowhere to be seen. Maybe upstairs or in the bathroom, but she definitely wasn't in the kitchen area with the other two.

Quietly, she set the pizza box down on the end table and took a careful step closer to the kitchen, making sure to avoid the squeaky floorboards. Technically, this was eavesdropping. She didn't love that she was listening in on someone else's conversation, but the apprehension she'd felt since seeing Ian's car in the driveway had only grown since coming inside. Something wasn't right here. She could feel it.

"Keep your voice down," Ian said in a low tone.

"What," the mystery woman replied. "You think she's going to hear us from upstairs?"

"No, but it's an old house. Sounds carry through the vents."

Quiet female laughter. The sound of it made Stella's skin crawl. No, this most definitely wasn't right.

"You've gotten paranoid, Ian," the woman said. "Is this what small-town living has done to you?"

Stella stood in the entryway, her heart beating in her throat. *Please don't*, she thought. She wasn't altogether sure what she was asking for. She just didn't want to be hurt. She didn't want Frances to be hurt. But her gut instinct told her that it was about to happen, anyway.

"I cannot believe what you're having to do to get your hands on this property," the woman half whispered. "Hat's off. I wouldn't be able to do it, even for an investment as good as this one."

"What am I doing?" Ian answered, half whispering, too. "Just putting the time in, Carter."

"This is more than putting time in, and you know it. Are you sure there's nothing else going on here?"

Stella realized she'd been holding her breath, and exhaled slowly. She was shaking. Her knees felt like jelly.

Ian was quiet. She could imagine him standing there, tall, dark and imposing. Was he giving this woman a knowing smile? Was he holding his index finger to his lips, reminding her again to keep her voice down?

All of a sudden, Stella felt sick to her stomach. *Carter.* This had to be his business partner. She was here to see the house for herself.

She sagged against the wall, feeling like someone had just kicked her in the ribs. And what had they told Frances? It couldn't have been the truth. Not with them whispering in the other room like this.

No, Frances was still supposed to believe that Ian was interested in buying the house for himself. Just like Stella was supposed to believe the same thing. She thought of him leaning down and kissing her. She thought of him smiling, and telling her exactly what she'd wanted to hear. *I want to live in it, Stella. And that's the truth.*

Angry tears stung the backs of her eyes. She'd let him in. She'd let him in, and it had only taken a little over a week. She'd let him convince her that he was being sincere about the house. And worse, that he was being sincere about her. At the end of the day, she had nobody to blame but herself. She'd known from the very beginning that Ian was only interested in what was best for Ian. She'd known it, and she'd chosen to ignore it. What was it that her mother had always told her? *Grow up, Stella. Get a clue.*

It looked like she hadn't grown up. She hadn't grown up at all.

"I found it!" Frances called from the top of the

stairs. "It wasn't in the closet with the other photo albums, so I had to dig around a little!"

Stella looked up to see Frances making her way down the steps. Beauregard bounded down past her, belly swinging, tail in the air like a flag.

When Frances saw her, she broke into a grin. "Stella!" she said. "I wasn't expecting you home so early."

Heat flooded Stella's cheeks. The jig was up now. Ian and Carter would realize she'd been standing there the entire time. They'd know that she overheard their conversation.

The smile on Frances's lips wilted, as she took the last few steps down the stairs.

"Honey?" she said. "What's wrong?"

"Stella…"

Slowly, she turned to see Ian standing there, pale as a sheet. A woman—tall, brunette and polished, the complete opposite of Stella's cozy, comfy, windswept look—was standing behind him, looking fairly uncomfortable.

"I can explain," he said.

It was laughable, really. Except, she couldn't bring herself to laugh. She couldn't bring herself to do anything but look up at him with her heart breaking inside her chest.

"I can't believe I let myself trust you."

"It's complicated."

"What's complicated about it? I asked you if you

were going to buy the house for yourself, and you said yes. That's what you told me."

Frances stared at them. "What's going on?"

"Were you *really* going to buy the house for yourself?" This, from Carter, who sounded incredulous.

Ian answered her without taking his eyes off Stella. "I wasn't going to, originally. But things have changed. Now..."

"That'll be on your dime," Carter said, her voice clipped. "The company would be officially out. Obviously."

"Would someone *please* tell me what's going on?" Frances said. Her hands were on her hips now.

"Ian lied to us," Stella said.

"Not to mention wasted my time," Carter mumbled underneath her breath.

"I didn't lie," Ian said. "I mean, I did, in the beginning. But now—"

"Now, what?" Stella bit out. "You've had a change of heart? It sure didn't sound like it a second ago."

"Ian," Frances said, turning to him. "Is this true?"

He rubbed his neck, looking for the most part like they'd backed him into a corner. Which Stella guessed they had. Every female in the room was looking at him for an explanation.

"Look," he said, his voice suddenly sharp. "You knew that I wanted the property. You both knew that. Of course I was going to tell you what you wanted to hear. At least at first."

Stella shook her head. "That's your version of clearing things up? That we should've known you'd be an asshole?"

Frances put a hand on her arm. "Stella—"

"No, Frances. He is." She glared up at him, her tone bitter. "You're right. I should've known better. The thing is, I *did* know better, but it seemed like you'd changed. You said all the right things, did all the right things."

"He was closing the deal," Carter said, quietly. A little condescendingly. "It's what we do."

"Don't help me," Ian said to her.

Frances sat down heavily on the stairs. "We can't be too angry, Stella," she said. "This was what these two weeks were for, remember? To find out if he was being sincere, and now we know."

Ian literally flinched at that. Stella supposed he'd never started out wanting to hurt them. And that he'd believed what he'd said in the beginning—that he would be doing her foster mother a favor by giving her so much for her house. But now? Now his trademark cockiness seemed to have vanished, leaving him looking unsure of himself for the first time since coming back to Christmas Bay.

Stella put her shoulders back. It didn't matter. It didn't matter if he was unsure, or sorry for leading them on. What's done was done. She was humiliated at how naive she'd been, but now that she knew the truth, she wouldn't make the same mistake twice. At least they'd found out his real intentions before they'd let the house go, and it had been torn down to make room for a luxury hotel or something.

"For what it's worth, Frances," Ian said, his voice low, "I'm sorry. I never saw it turning out this way. And, Stella…"

She crossed her arms over her chest. "Save it, Ian."

"So, there's nothing I can say to convince you to listen to me."

"I've spent the last week listening to you. So, no. There's really nothing you can say."

His expression hardened. "Okay. I get it. Just like when we were kids. You've made up your mind about me, so screw it, right?"

Despite everything, her heart squeezed. They had a shared history. Once upon a time, they'd both been damaged, angry kids, who'd felt like nobody loved them. Who'd felt like everyone knew everything about them by the way they dressed, or what side of town they'd come from. Stella knew what it was like to be judged. And Ian had been judged plenty back then. But he'd brought so much of that on himself. Just like he'd brought this on himself today. If he wanted people to give him a chance, he should stop treating them like dirt. As far as she was concerned, it was that simple. Not to mention, he was probably manipulating her right this minute. He knew exactly what was in her heart, despite her trying her best to hide it from him.

She raised her chin, gazing up at him. He wasn't going to manipulate her this time. He wasn't going to manipulate her ever again.

"Okay, then," he said quietly. "We'll go."

Carter grabbed her purse, looking like she couldn't wait to leave. Stella knew they'd probably have it out in the car, if the expression on her face was any indication. She'd probably been manipulated by him, too. Apparently, nobody was safe in Ian's orbit.

He stared down at Stella for another few seconds, then visibly set his jaw. The muscles bunched with tension.

And then he stepped around her and headed for the door.

"Ian," Frances said.

He stopped in his tracks. Then he slowly turned to face her.

"No matter what," she said, "I'll always love you."

His face was a mask. Completely emotionless. Stella knew him well enough by now to know this mask was worn out of necessity. No matter what he was feeling, he wasn't going to show it. She remembered that look from when he was a teenager, walking out the door of Frances's house for the last time. She'd said something similar back then. And he'd looked at her much the same way he was looking at her now. He was shut down. In the deepest throes of protecting himself.

The problem was, she didn't know what was behind that mask. She thought she'd started catching a glimpse over the last week, but she'd been wrong. It was possible that Ian would never be capable of true emotion or empathy. It was possible that he was simply too damaged, unable to love or be loved in any kind of meaningful way.

The thought was enough to make her want to cry. Not out of anger or frustration. But out of sadness for the loss of something that had never really materialized in the first place.

As she watched him open the door for Carter and then follow her out, she knew that no matter how betrayed she felt, she would probably mourn that loss for a while.

Chapter Ten

Ian pulled up to the motel, where mismatched Christmas lights blinked in the office window and Carter's rental car was parked out front. A white, hardtop convertible. A laughable choice for the Oregon Coast in December. But it was a nice car, and Carter was used to the best.

He put the Porsche into Park and cut the engine. The silence between them was heavy and tense. He hadn't said a word since they'd left Frances's house, and Carter hadn't pushed. She knew better than that.

But she turned to him now, the leather seat squeaking underneath her, and fixed him with a hard look.

"Okay, Ian," she said. "Want to tell me what the hell is going on?"

He grit his teeth and looked out the window to the

dark outline of the mountains beyond. There was a full moon tonight, peeking through the clouds overhead, and it bathed everything in silver. He couldn't see the ocean from here, but he could imagine how beautiful it would look underneath the moonlight.

Ian had always prided himself on seeing everything so clearly. He knew exactly what he wanted, and he knew how to get it. But since coming back to Christmas Bay, he'd been fumbling over things that had once been easy for him. He'd never had an issue lying to people before, if it was for a good reason. He'd believed that misleading Stella and Frances, and the rest of their family, had been for a good reason. Frances would end up with a ton of money, and so would he when he resold the property, and that was that.

But getting caught tonight, and the *way* he'd gotten caught, with Stella hearing him talking so coldly about the house and his plan to get it, was affecting him in ways that he was still trying to get his head around. It hadn't settled yet. He felt so out of sorts that he didn't even know how to answer Carter now. *Yeah, I was planning on buying this property for my own gain, but I ended up falling in love, and that's making me face what kind of person I am, and I don't like what I see.*

He couldn't say that to her. He couldn't even say that to himself. Not without some serious reflection, and honestly, that scared the hell out of him.

"I've been having second thoughts," he said, his voice grave. "That's all."

She watched him. "So, I was right. I knew there was something you weren't telling me."

"Yeah, you were right."

"Can I ask why?"

He swallowed hard. How much should he say? Carter was his business partner, and they'd known each other a long time. But having heart-to-hearts wasn't their style. The reason they worked so well together was that they had similar personalities. They didn't get caught up on sentimental snags. They were quick and efficient, and saved the emotion for their personal lives. Although, in Ian's case, he'd never had much of that to spare. Jill had muttered that under her breath once. That he was cold. Was that what he was?

Taking a deep breath, he looked over at her. In the dark, the angles of her face looked sharper and more severe. Carter was an attractive woman, and she worked hard at keeping herself up. He didn't think he'd ever seen her without makeup before. So different from Stella, who radiated a natural, bohemian beauty. She was a coastal girl, through and through. Just another example of how everything in his life had seemed to collide in the last few days. His life in San Francisco and his existence in Christmas Bay were about as opposite as they could possibly be, and now they were mixing in the most bizarre kind of way.

He licked his lips, which were chapped from the fishing trip. He knew his face was windburned, too. He probably looked like a million damn bucks right about now, complete with the scruff on his jaw.

"You knew I grew up here," he said.

She nodded.

"And that I was in foster care for a few years."

"I knew that."

"Frances was my foster mother. Stella's, too."

Carter watched him, her eyes looking darker than usual in the gritty parking lot light. "Oh," she finally said. "Ian... I'm sorry."

"There's nothing to be sorry for. She was a really nice lady, and I screwed it up, like I had a tendency to do as a kid. Fast-forward fifteen years, and I saw an easy opportunity for a sale. An older woman with Alzheimer's, who's got a sentimental attachment to her house, blah, blah, blah. She wanted to sell it to someone who was going to live there and raise a family, so that's what I told her I was going to do. Pretty cut-and-dried, right?"

Carter didn't say anything. Just sat there watching him like he was getting ready to explode or something. He wasn't used to her handling him with kid gloves like this. It made him feel like he *was* about to explode.

He cleared his throat. "Only it wasn't cut-and-dried at all. Because I didn't think I cared as much as I apparently do."

"Of course you care," she said quietly. "You'd have to be a robot not to care."

"Well, then. That's what I've been all these years. Because I've never had this problem before. Only it looks like caring *is* a problem, because now they hate me."

"Um, no. That's not what it looked like to me."

"How can you say that? Especially Stella."

"She doesn't feel like she can trust you, but she doesn't hate you. Anyone can see that. In fact, if I had to guess, I'd say she probably loves you."

He shook his head. "No. Love doesn't happen in a week."

"Of course it does. But that's not really the point, because you've known each other a lot longer than that."

It was true, they had. But he'd never really wanted to acknowledge how he felt about Stella back then, because that would mean taking a harder look at a lot of things.

"I'm sorry I didn't tell you sooner that I've been going back and forth on the house."

Carter shrugged. Unlike Stella, she wasn't going to take this personally. To her, it was business, and business deals fell through all the time. "It's fine," she said. "We have all the property we can handle, anyway. But can I ask you a question?"

"Shoot."

"If you buy it, are you seriously going to live here?"

She said it with such an incredulous look on her

face that he could clearly see, even in the dim light of the car. Carter was not the small-town type. She probably thought he'd lost his damn mind even contemplating this.

He smiled. "I'm a long way from that. But the truth is, I don't know what I'm going to do yet. If I do decide to make an offer, Frances might tell me to go straight to hell. She won't trust me now, and I can hardly blame her for that."

Carter watched him matter-of-factly. "Then get her to trust you."

"I was trying, remember? It didn't work."

"You were trying by deceiving them. Try being sincere, and see how far that gets you."

He looked over at the Christmas lights flashing in the motel office window. If only it were that easy.

"She might hear me out," he said. "Maybe. But Stella won't. No way."

"This is not the Ian Steele I know," Carter said with a sigh. "If you want something, you go get it. You always have. Why should this be any different?"

He let his gaze settle on her again. "Because this time, I don't know if I deserve it."

The car was starting to get cold, and he felt his body tense. It would only get colder. Fog would probably roll in tonight, blanketing the town in its freezing mist. Christmas was so close now. He never thought he'd be feeling this way, having this kind of

conversation. He never thought he'd be back here, period. Where all his most complicated memories were.

Carter folded her hands in her lap and looked over
at him in the darkness. The blinking lights from the
office illuminated her face, and then cast it in shadow
again. The moment felt surreal, like he was dreaming. He felt like he'd come to a strange crossroads,
and he was choosing which way to turn.

"We all deserve a second chance, Ian," she said
softly. "All of us."

Stella unlocked the door of the candy shop, her
heart heavy inside her chest. Frances had wanted to
talk after Ian and Carter had left last night, but Stella
hadn't trusted herself not to cry. She'd felt too emotional, and too embarrassed about that, to be able
to have any kind of meaningful conversation in the
moment. So, she'd kissed her foster mother on the
cheek and gone upstairs to draw a hot bath. She'd
ended up crying herself to sleep.

She stood at the glass door now, tucking the keys
back into the pocket of her cardigan, feeling like the
biggest fool that had ever walked the earth. She knew
at the end of the day it was Ian who'd lied. But she
still felt responsible for letting it get this far. How
could she have been so stupid?

But even as she thought it, she knew exactly how
it had gotten this far. She'd let herself fall in love
with him, that's how. And there was no point deny-

ing it anymore, no point telling herself some kind of story to rationalize that feeling away. It was what it was. She'd fallen in love, or maybe she'd always been in love. He'd sensed that vulnerability and like a pit viper had been getting ready to strike.

She took a deep breath, willing back the prickling behind her eyes. This feeling of being utterly crushed had to do with more than just Ian, she knew that. It was everything all at once. It was having to come to terms with Frances's memory loss, and what her future would look like if it wasn't going to be in the house they all loved. It had to do with Stella's history there, and how she'd come to live with Frances in the first place. As the daughter of a woman who hadn't cared about her at all—a woman who'd broken her heart.

It was everything. And it was also Ian. How could it not be, after he'd swept into town, all rich and handsome, like Prince Charming himself? She'd thought she hated him. She'd thought she'd be able to resist him if he set his sights on her, but she'd been wrong about that.

Now she just had to pick herself back up and dust herself off. This wasn't the end of the world, even if it had felt pretty close last night. This was just another example of people being people, and if she'd learned anything over the years, it was that people rarely surprised her for the better. Even the rich, handsome ones.

She tucked her hair behind her ears and turned toward the supply closet. She'd distract herself this morning. The candy bins always needed cleaning, and the more she cleaned, the less she could think about Ian. At least, she hoped so, anyway.

Behind her, the bell above the door dinged, and she turned to greet her first customer of the day with a determined smile.

But as soon as she saw who was standing there, she felt herself stiffen, as if facing a sudden, harsh wind.

"Ian," she said, her voice cold. "What are you doing here?"

He was wearing a sweatshirt and jeans, and looked so different that she had to work not to stare. She didn't think he even owned a pair of jeans, let alone a sweatshirt. She'd never seen him like this before, looking so down to earth with his hair a little messy, and the stubble on his jaw thicker than last night. The truth was, he'd never been sexier, and her body reacted accordingly. Her belly tightened and her pulse skipped, which made her angry.

"I need to talk to you," he said.

"There's nothing to say."

"Of course there's something to say."

She retreated behind the counter. She needed a physical barrier between them. Her heart was pounding too hard not to have one.

"If I hadn't come home when I did," she bit out,

"would you have just kept lying to Frances last night? Making her think she'd be selling to a friend?"

He frowned, and he looked older then. He didn't look arrogant, or even particularly confident. He just looked tired.

"I'm not going to lie to you anymore," he said. "I'm going to be completely honest, which I realize you might have a hard time believing."

She pursed her lips.

"I'm not sure what I would've done last night," he continued. "I do know what I would do today. I'd come clean. I'd stop this whole stupid charade, because I realize how much it hurt you."

"Would you have ever come to that conclusion on your own, Ian?" she asked tightly. "Did it have to come to this?"

"I don't know. But I'd been having second thoughts…"

"When was that? When we kissed?" She felt a terrible ache rise in her throat. "Or was that just another part of the lie?"

"My feelings for you surprised me, Stella."

She didn't answer. She found she couldn't, without risking her voice cracking.

"I'm not proud of this," he continued quietly. "But I wasn't planning on coming back here and caring about much of anything. And then, I got to know you again. I got to spend some time with Frances and your family. And everything I thought I knew about myself got turned upside down. Can you understand that?"

She could. But she didn't want to admit it out loud. She was too hurt for that. Too mad. So she crossed her arms over her chest and looked away.

The silence in the candy shop settled between them. Stella didn't know whether to hope a customer would come in and interrupt, or whether to pray they'd be alone for a little while longer. It all felt so delicate, like the tiniest thing might shatter the moment. Maybe it needed shattering. But maybe it needed saving.

"I want to earn your trust back," Ian finally said, his voice gravelly.

She stared up at him. "Why?"

"So you can get to know me. Not the me who was trying to trick you. The me that I'm still trying to get to know myself."

There was something about that—the words, the tone of his voice—that made her heart flutter. Could she ever trust him again? Why would she need to? He'd be leaving Christmas Bay soon, she knew that. If he wasn't going to buy the house, there was nothing to keep him here.

"Why, Ian?" she asked. "What's the point?"

"I don't want to leave it like this. And for me, the house isn't off the table yet."

"So you can tear it down? Build on the property?"

"No," he said firmly.

"Then, what?"

"I don't know yet. But I want to stay, like I was planning. Until Christmas Eve. And then, you can tell Frances what you really think of me. For real this time."

She resisted the urge to laugh at that. It was all so ridiculous. He didn't have a prayer of convincing her that he was being sincere. That ship had sailed.

But even so, even with that old, familiar defensiveness forming inside her chest, she knew there was still a small part of her that wanted to believe him. *Probably the part that's so attracted to him*, she thought dismally.

"There are so many houses," she said. "*So* many. Why this one? Why us?"

"I don't know that I can answer that yet. And it's not because I don't want to. I just don't know why myself. But I'm guessing it's because I've spent so much time trying to convince myself that my childhood happened a certain way. That there were certain people to blame for it. My mother was definitely part of that story. But there were other people, like you and Frances, Kyla and Marley, my aunt…that I need to untangle from the narrative."

She nodded slowly. "So, staying here until Christmas Eve would be therapeutic for you."

"In a way. Yes. I think it would."

She couldn't argue with that. She'd found that to be true herself. Since coming home again, she'd had to come to terms with a lot of things. It wasn't easy, but it needed to happen. She'd known that for a very long time, but hadn't had the courage to take that first step until Frances had needed her. And now, here she was.

"Okay," she said. "But what if we end up right back at square one? What if I can't trust you, Ian?"

"Then I walk away for good. House be damned."

There was a look in his eyes that said he meant it. And something about that left her cold. If he walked away for good, how was she going to untangle him from her own story? How was she going to untangle him from her heart?

She nodded again. "Alright," she said. "Until Christmas Eve, then."

He watched her, his expression unreadable. She wondered if she was the worst kind of fool. Or, if she was doing the right thing in giving him another chance. Frances would say it was the Christian thing to do, and of course, that's how she would see it. Frances saw every cloud with a silver lining wrapped neatly around it.

He'd be leaving soon. Less than a week. Honestly, how much damage could he do in that amount of time?

Plenty, she answered herself, as her gaze fell to his mouth. To his lips that she'd kissed just a few short days ago.

Plenty.

* * *

Ian pulled the Porsche into what he now thought of as his parking space—the one kitty-corner to the front office—and cut the engine. From here he could see the ocean in the distance, grumpy and churning this morning. The weather in Christmas Bay changed so fast, almost morphing with his mood some days. And his mood today was heavy, like the sea.

He ran his hands down his thighs. He'd woken up at the god-awful hour of four thirty, when the entire world seemed unconscious, and hadn't been able to go back to sleep. He'd done Wordle, something Jill had gotten him hooked on, and then had spent the next few hours watching the clock, until he'd known Coastal Sweets would be open. He'd driven down there with an entire speech in mind. He was going to lay it on thick with Stella. He was going to charm her, working himself back into her good graces with a few well-chosen sentences and a practiced nuance to his demeanor. He knew how to handle people. She was no exception.

Except, as he'd parked his car in front of the candy shop, he'd known that she actually *was* an exception, and all the crap he'd planned on laying on her wasn't going to work. What's more, he didn't want it to work. He didn't want to be dealing in crap at all, least of all with Stella Clarke.

So, where did that leave him? Confused as hell. He'd walked into the shop wearing clothes that he might as well have rolled out of bed in—and basically had—and told her the truth. That he wanted to stay, and that he wanted her to trust him again.

And since Christmas miracles never ceased, she didn't throw him out on his ass. She'd listened, albeit with that familiar go-to-hell expression on her pretty face, but she'd listened. And then he'd gotten into his car again and driven back to the motel, wondering why it was so important that he'd bought himself this time. Was it because he really was thinking about buying the house for himself, and he wanted to get a handle on that and what it would mean in the long run? Or was it because he simply didn't want to leave yet? Figuring this out was truly going to take some time. But months in Christmas Bay, or even years, wouldn't do the trick for Ian and his messed-up psyche.

He sat in the Porsche now with his heart beating painfully inside his chest. He guessed it all came down to what kind of person he wanted to be. And he'd never taken the time to ask that question of himself before. He'd certainly never taken the time to answer it. What kind of man did he want to be? The kind who would snatch up houses from sweet grandma-types, just to make a profit? Or the kind who looked inside himself, and attempted to change for the better?

Slowly, he opened the door and climbed out of the car, feeling ten years older. Last night with Carter, this morning with Stella—it had all seeped into his bones until he felt like they might snap from the tension, from the heaviness there.

"Good morning, Mr. Steele!"

He looked over to see Loretta heading into the office. She was struggling to push the door open with her hip, while balancing a stack of ever-present towels in her arms.

He rushed over to help her.

"Good morning," he said, reaching over her head to push the door open. "Have your hands full?"

"Just a smidge."

It wasn't until then that he looked down and saw that she'd been crying. Her mascara was smudged underneath her eyes, and her nose was red and drippy.

He frowned. "What's wrong?"

She walked through the door and set the towels on the front counter. Sniffing, she plucked a tissue from a box next to the telephone.

"Well, my grandson is in the hospital," she said, and then honked into the tissue. "How do you like that?"

"Oh… I'm sorry, Loretta. What's wrong with him?"

"It's the asthma. Normally we can keep it under control, but he got a respiratory virus, and those always make the asthma worse. Sometimes he ends up in the ER."

Ian put a hand on her shoulder. He wasn't sure if she'd mind the contact, but he'd touched her before he could think better of it. Not like him. It was like he was morphing into someone he didn't recognize anymore.

"Is he going to be okay?" he asked.

She tossed the tissue into the trash. "He'll be alright, thank goodness. But my daughter lost her job last week. Her company is downsizing, and now she has no insurance." She sniffed and smiled up at him gamely. "Look at me, going on and on, probably embarrassing you. Things could be worse. That's what my mother always used to say. 'Now, Loretta, things could be worse!' And they could, they really, really could."

But the way her eyes were filling with fresh tears wasn't convincing him that she completely bought into this logic. Things seemed to be pretty bad at the moment, even if they *could* be worse.

"I'm sorry," she said. "I'm not usually this emotional. I think it's just because Christmas is coming up, and we're on a tight budget. You know."

He really didn't know. Ian wasn't used to budgeting squat.

"Anyway." She shook her head, and her snow flake earrings swung next to her face. It seemed like she had a different pair of Christmas earrings for every day of the week. "How are *you*? You said you were going to be here until the holidays, so we get to keep you around a little longer. How's your lady friend?"

It took him a minute to realize she was talking about Stella. She hadn't forgotten her from the day she'd picked him up to go to the diner outside town.

He smiled and put his hands in his pockets. "She's fine. Nothing to report there."

"I see. Well, you never know." She winked at him like she might know something he didn't. He doubted it. Although he'd like nothing more than to kiss Stella again—actually, he'd like to do much more than kiss her—but he didn't think she'd let him touch her again after last night. A cold, hard reality that made him swallow with some difficulty now. The regret, the sudden sadness, was overwhelming.

"Oh, I'm sorry," Loretta said, suddenly looking flustered. "Is that presumptuous of me? I always do that. I always want to matchmake, and I forget it's none of my business. Another thing my mother used to say. 'It's none of your beeswax, Loretta!'"

"It's fine," he said. "It's a small town, and you're just being friendly. I understand wanting a happily-ever-after for people."

He couldn't believe he'd just said that. He didn't think he'd ever used that term in his entire life. But there was a first time for everything.

"Yes, I guess that's me in a nutshell," Loretta said. "Always wanting a happily-ever-after. The most important thing is family and friends, right? What's a hospital bill in the grand scheme of things?"

He knew that was a very Pollyanna way of looking at it. A big hospital bill could be catastrophic for a lot of families. He wondered how much of this Loretta really believed, or if it was just a way of her being able to get through the tough times. Maybe it was a little bit of both. Faith, with a hefty dose of perseverance on the side.

"Well," she said, patting his hand. "Thank you for opening the door for me. I probably would've dropped my clean towels all over the parking lot if you hadn't come along when you had."

"Don't sell yourself short. I've seen you balance a lot more than that."

She laughed. "Next stop, the circus, right? I'll have to perfect my tightrope routine."

"I'd be first in line." He paused then, watching her closely. "Are you sure you're alright?"

She waved him away. "Fine, fine. But thank you for asking. You have a wonderful day, Mr. Steele."

"You too, Loretta."

And as he walked out the door, fishing his room card out of his back pocket, he wondered again how okay she really was. Faith could only get you so far when your bills were piling up.

Chapter Eleven

Stella trailed along behind Frances at the Methodist Church Christmas Bazaar, half-heartedly running her hand along the quilts as she passed. She'd promised Frances she'd come this morning, but all she could think about was Ian. In fact, she hadn't been able to stop thinking about him since he'd come into the shop yesterday, asking for another chance. He'd left her feeling more confused than ever.

"What about this one?" Frances asked, pointing to an adorable pink and yellow quilt on a rack. She was shopping for Marley and the baby. She wanted something Marley could wrap Emily up in and rock her to sleep on especially chilly days. Something cozy and cheerful. They'd come to the right place. The church bazaar was bursting with beautiful hand-made items for Christmas. In fact, Stella wished they had more than one baby to shop for.

"Oh, that's pretty," she said. "I love the yellow. It's so buttery."

Frances picked up the corner and ran her fingertips along the stitching. "Will you look at that? That's hand stitched. It must've taken forever."

Stella nodded, hearing her but not really hearing her. She was distracted but trying her hardest not to show it.

"Honey," Frances said, putting the quilt down again. "What's wrong?"

Stella smiled. "Nothing."

"That's not true."

She'd been trying to steer clear of what happened with Ian the other night. She and Frances had finally talked about it, but going over it again and again would just be upsetting for them both. And Frances had started forgetting the details, anyway. They were foggy in her memory now, and that's probably how they needed to stay. It was less painful that way.

Still, she fixed Stella with a hard look. She was wearing another one of her famous Christmas sweatshirts this morning. This one having come from this very bazaar last year.

"It's Ian, isn't it?" Frances asked.

Stella put her hands in her jacket pockets. Her stomach growled. The entire place smelled like baked goods. More specifically, it smelled like the plump cinnamon rolls that were sitting on the next table over, frosting oozing down their sides and pooling onto their red and green paper plates. She was starving. She'd skipped breakfast, and she *never* skipped breakfast. Maybe this thing with Ian was affecting her more than she thought.

She nodded. "Yes."

"Come here."

Frances reached for her hand and led her to a few foldout chairs by the window where there were less people milling about. Stella sat beside her and watched as a couple of little girls played tag around their frazzled mother.

"This isn't just about the house, is it?" Frances asked.

Stella looked down at her hands in her lap. What could she say to that but the truth? Frances probably knew how she felt about Ian, anyway. It was most likely written all over her face.

"No," she said. "It isn't."

"You have feelings for him."

It wasn't a question.

Stella nodded.

"What are you going to do about that?"

"What do you mean?"

"I mean, what are you going to do, Stella? Let him go back to San Francisco without telling him how you feel?"

Stella shook her head. "It's not that simple."

"Why?"

"Well, for starters, he lied to us."

"Yes, he did. And that was a rotten thing to do. But he also apologized."

"After he got caught."

"You can look at it that way if you want, but I don't think that's being completely fair to him."

Stella shifted in her chair, incredulous. "Why are you still defending him?"

"I'm not excusing what he did. But I also know that he's used to keeping people at an arm's length. It's exactly what he did as a boy, and he's still doing it. It might look a little different now, all dressed up in a real estate deal, but it's the same kind of behavior. He's hurting. He's been hurting this whole time, and he doesn't know how to get close to anyone." Frances shrugged. "That's my professional opinion, anyway, thanks to all my years taking in kids. And I know a thing or two about you, too, Stella."

"Oh?" Stella looked away. She wasn't sure she wanted to hear this. Mostly because Frances was usually right.

"Ian might have a hard time being honest and getting close, but you have a hard time forgiving anyone for wronging you. And I understand why. Your experience with your mom taught you to be very cautious, and I can't blame you for that. You've learned the hardest way a person can learn that human beings are awful to each other. But I'm worried that by always expecting the worst in people, you're not able to see the good in them, too."

"I don't think Ian's a bad person…"

"No, you wouldn't. But you're not seeing the *entire* person, either."

"But—"

"I know." Frances held up a hand. "He lied to us. But when does that stop becoming a thing that he did, and start becoming an excuse for you?"

Stella felt the blood rush to her face. Frances had never pulled many punches. She never let any of her girls get away with telling themselves stories. It wasn't productive, she always said. *Honesty above all else.* Which was ironic, since they were talking about Ian, here.

But she had a point. She had a very good point. Stella had known for a long time that this was an issue of hers. She had a hard time letting things go. Forgiving was a fine art that she hadn't mastered yet.

She wondered now how it would feel to forgive her mother for all the misery she'd put her through. She wondered if it would be freeing, like it was for all those people she'd seen on talk show panels over the years. Talking about forgiveness and wringing their hands in their laps, while the audience looked on sympathetically.

Thinking about it hurt her brain. She didn't know where to begin to consider forgiveness. It was a big word, with even bigger implications. If she started letting things go, did that mean lowering her defenses, too? And how would that look in the long run? She imagined herself as an old lady, surrounded by friends and family, some of whom she'd forgiven and let back into her life again. It was a nice picture. But was it realistic?

She looked over at Frances, who was watching her closely.

"You have to ask yourself," Frances said softly, "is it worth letting Ian in? Is it worth the chance of getting hurt again? Personally, I'd take the risk. You might be missing out on something amazing if you don't."

Stella ran her hands down her thighs. "I told him I'd give him a chance. He's staying until the Flotilla…"

"That's a start, honey," Frances said. "But what are you going to do in the meantime?"

"Are you saying I should make the first move?"

"No. I'm simply telling you not to be afraid of making the first move. Pursue this, if you think it can make you happy. You have no idea where it might end up."

Stella considered this. Frances was right. Again. If she was truly going to give Ian a second chance, and let him prove himself to her, and to all of them, then she didn't want to sit around waiting. She didn't want to be passive. She wanted to be an active participant in whatever ended up happening to her and her family.

"I haven't heard from him today," she said slowly.

"Maybe I'll go over sometime this weekend, see if he wants to get a coffee, and talk a little bit."

Frances patted her hand. "That's my girl. This doesn't mean you're being any less shrewd about him. It just means you're being less jaded, and that's a very good thing."

Was it? Stella didn't know yet. But at the end of the day, she supposed this chance that she was giving Ian could be a chance for her, too. It could be a turning point, if she let it. A moment to learn and grow, even if things didn't turn out exactly how she hoped they would. And that was a good feeling. Much better than what she was used to—which was carrying around the weight of suspicion every day of her life.

"I almost forgot," Frances said.

Her foster mother reached inside her tote bag and pulled out a glossy magazine. Stella recognized it immediately—it was the newest issue of *Coastal Monthly*. The issue with their story in it.

"I wanted to bring you a copy," Frances continued. "Gwen dropped a few off last night. The article is a keeper. The pictures are even better. The house looks so beautiful. I'm so proud of it."

Her eyes grew misty then, and Stella leaned forward to give her a hug. Her sweet foster mother. Facing the unknown on so many fronts. The house, her memory, her future. But one thing was certain—she wasn't going to have to face them alone.

* * *

Stella sat in the Jeep with the engine running and the heater blowing against her cheeks. She'd just dropped Frances off at the house, and had told her she was going to run a few errands. She needed to go to the grocery store and the credit union, but the presence of the magazine on the seat beside her had proved to be too much of a distraction. She'd pulled over next to the fire station, where a cheerful antique fire truck was parked out front—complete with a Christmas wreath on the grill—and picked up the issue with her heart in her throat.

It was hard to believe Ian had shown up for this interview only a little over a week ago. It felt like he'd been a part of their lives for a lot longer than that. Which, of course, he had been. But the problem was, Stella had begun thinking of Ian Steele as two separate people. There was the kid who'd lived with them for two years and had made that time fairly awful for everyone. And then there was the man who'd shown up here, working his way back into her heart after all this time.

She stared down at the magazine in her hands. Frances's beautiful old Victorian had made the cover. It was so lovely—frozen in time in the photograph, perched on the edge of the cliffs of Cape Longing, with its sparkling Christmas tree in the bay window.

Her heart ached at the sight of it. Frances's home. Stella's and Marley's and Kyla's home. And Ian's home, too. Whether or not he wanted to claim it as that, it absolutely was.

She opened the cover and flipped through the slick pages until she came to the featured story. The story about the three-story gingerbread house on the cape, that was once rumored to be haunted, and was now about to be on the market for the first time in generations.

Settling back in her seat, she took a sip of her coffee, and began to read.

Ian stood on the deserted stretch of beach and stared up at the house at the top of the cliffs. He'd taken his shoes off and was holding them in his hands, along with his wadded-up socks. He knew he'd never be able to get the sand off his feet to be able to put them back on again, but that was fine. He didn't care.

He'd spent the last twenty-four hours unplugged from the world, trying for some much-needed perspective after seeing Stella at the candy shop yesterday. He wanted her to trust him again, but he'd left her realizing he wanted more than that. And he needed time to figure out what that was.

He'd called Carter and told her he'd be unavailable for a while, and to send him an SOS if it was an emergency. She'd laughed, seemingly unsurprised by the whole thing, and had asked when he was moving back to Christmas Bay.

She'd been joking, of course. But now that he was

standing here, with the frigid waters of the Pacific lapping at his feet, he wondered if she'd had some kind of inkling, deep, deep down. She'd always been intuitive that way.

He wasn't planning on anything that drastic. But still… He'd been doing some thinking, dare he say, meditating on it for hours now, and had found himself in an almost trancelike state. He felt more calm, more peaceful than he had in years. Jill would be proud. She was always going on and on about her yoga, saying it centered her. He'd dismissed that as new age nonsense. He went running and lifted weights. That's what centered him.

But he'd been wrong about that, he realized now. Like he'd been wrong about so many other things in his life. It was as if his time in Christmas Bay had scrubbed him clean, and he could finally see the world without the cloud of bitterness that he'd always viewed it through before.

And why was that? If he had to guess, it was mostly because of Stella. He'd let himself fall for her—a woman who scared him to death. She scared him because she was everything he wasn't—loyal, kind, down to earth, good to the core. He'd wanted to see those qualities as weaknesses before. But now, he saw them as absolute strengths. She was a good person. And she'd seen something in him that he'd been slow to see himself.

He was still looking this afternoon. He'd come

down to the beach to walk barefoot on the sand, something he hadn't done just for the sake of doing it since middle school. And now, as he looked up at the house, he thought about his past without fighting it. He wondered how things might've been different for him if he'd had a safe place to go when he was little. Safe people to turn to, who might've understood his situation. The trauma of being stuck in a house full of turbulence and discontent. Having somewhere to go, somewhere to *be*, might've changed everything for him.

Of course, hindsight was twenty-twenty. It was easy to look back now and see all the things that could've gone differently. Still, though. It was something to think about, something to chew on. He might not be able to go back and save that angry boy with the bruises on his arms and the holes in his sneakers, but he might be able to do something for other kids like him.

Maybe. Just maybe.

Stella knocked on room 128 with butterflies in her stomach. The wind kept blowing her hair all over the place, and she grabbed it with one hand. She should've pulled it back before getting out of the Jeep, but the last thing on her mind had been her hair.

Now, as she turned to look for Ian's car in the parking lot, her thoughts came back to the article again. More specifically, the picture of Ian and Frances on the widow's walk that day. He'd been so handsome, so full of himself with his pricey clothes and superior demeanor. She hadn't been able to stand him. But now? Now, she was being forced to take another look at that day, through the lens of a woman who'd let down her guard, for better or worse.

She pulled the sea air into her lungs, trying to slow her pulse, which had been racing ever since she'd decided to drive over here. Ever since she'd read his interview with Gwen, who'd quoted him saying something that wouldn't leave her alone. It kept coming back to her over and over again, like the words to a song that you couldn't get out of your head. *I loved this place as a kid*, he'd said. *I just didn't know* how *to love it.* He'd gone on to explain why he'd made up the story about the ghost, and why he'd spread it around, and had even touched on his life after leaving foster care with Frances. But it was those two little sentences that Stella couldn't stop thinking about. Because it was exactly how she felt about Ian himself.

"Hello, there!"

Startling, Stella turned to see a woman standing a few yards away. She was wearing a Christmas sweater that would rival any of Frances's.

"Are you looking for Mr. Steele?" the woman asked.

"Actually, I am."

"Well, that makes two of us." She stepped forward and held out her hand, then gave what Stella thought was a wobbly smile. "Loretta Dwight. I work in the front office."

"Nice to meet you."

"I don't usually keep tabs on our guests like this, but I really need to find him."

"Oh…" Stella frowned. "Is there an emergency?"

"No, no. Nothing like that, but I do need to talk to him."

Stella watched her, curious.

"Are you two friends?" Loretta asked, looking hopeful. Almost desperate for an answer. "Are you the one who picked him up the other day?"

"I am," she said. "But I don't—"

"Then you know him pretty well?"

"I…"

"Because I think he might be the kindest, most wonderful man I've met in a long time."

Stella stared down at the woman. She was petite, with poofy hair and a sweet way about her. She reminded her of Frances. But it was what she'd just said about Ian that had Stella practically frozen in place. *Kind? Wonderful?* It was true that he'd seemed to change over the last few days, but this was an interesting take for a relative stranger.

"I'm sorry?" she managed.

Loretta's eyes filled with tears. "Oh, no. Here I go again. I've been doing this all afternoon."

"Crying?" Stella asked. "What did he do?"

"Nothing! Well, that's not true. He did something.

These are happy tears. They just keep coming, like I've sprung a leak or something."

"I'm sorry," Stella said. "I'm so confused…"

Loretta laughed, digging a tissue from her pocket. "Of course you are, sweetie. Look at me, going on like this. The reason I wanted to see if you were friends was because I thought you could help me track him down. I've been waiting for him to come back to the motel, but he's been gone all day, and I just need to thank him. I need to thank him for what he did for our family."

Stella waited, a warm feeling blooming inside her chest. "Oh?"

Loretta wiped her eyes with the tissue. "He gave us a wonderful Christmas present," she said. "And I just want to give him a hug."

Ian waited at the front desk inside Weatherly Court, as the receptionist picked up the phone to call his aunt's room. Apparently, she'd been feeling a little under the weather, and had been getting her meals delivered. The receptionist, Katie, according to her nametag, said they usually wouldn't disturb her, but would make an exception for Ian, since he was from out of town.

She gave him a flirty smile while the phone rang. He was used to this kind of thing. Mostly because he put out flirty, overly confident vibes himself. *She's not feeling great? No problem, because I'm rich and powerful, and the rules don't apply to me, anyway. Wink, wink.*

It was only now, while he stood there with his hands in his slacks pockets, that he realized he should probably stop doing that. It was douchey. Instead, he could just be a decent guy and ask politely, and see where that got him.

Clenching his jaw, he thought about his aunt. Picturing her all by herself, elderly and sick, with nothing but the television to keep her company. He hoped her situation wasn't that depressing, but it might be, and then what?

"Betty?" the receptionist said into her headpiece. "It's Katie at the front desk. How are you feeling today?"

Ian watched her as she doodled a bubbly heart on her message pad.

"Oh, that's good to hear. Well, there's someone here to see you. Are you up for a visitor?"

Silence. A couple of women shuffled by, and he nodded hello. One of them wore a visor that said World's Best Grandma! She smiled at him, and he smiled back.

"Oh, good," Katie said. "Well, he'll be waiting in the lobby by the fireplace, okay? Okay, hon. See you soon. Bye-bye."

She hung up and gazed up at Ian. "She'll be down in a few. She just has to grab a sweater. She's feeling much better today."

He felt his shoulders relax a little. He hadn't realized how tense he'd been until just now. He was nervous enough to see her again and have to explain himself after all this time. But he wasn't sure he would've been able to live with himself if she seemed miserable on top of it.

"Oh, good," he said. "Thank you for calling her."

"No problem. So, you're her nephew?" she asked. "What a nice surprise. I know she'll be thrilled."

He wasn't so sure about that. She was elderly; she wasn't stupid. Would she want to welcome him back into her life? Someone who had left it so carelessly?

He'd know soon enough.

He walked over to the gas fireplace, where there were several cushiony chairs and a cozy-looking couch. There was a fresh pine wreath hanging over the brick hearth, making the small space smell like Christmas. Coffee percolated in a pot to his right, and he contemplated pouring himself a cup, but decided against it. He didn't need caffeine in the mix— his heart was beating fast enough as it was. He'd once met with the vice president of a billion dollar tech company about a property on the beach. Millions and millions of dollars had hung in the balance, and that was less stressful than this right here.

He sat on the edge of the couch, watching the bright orange flames lick the air. Their heat radiated against his skin. It felt good. He had a fireplace in his high-rise condo, but he rarely used it. Actually, now that he thought about it, his condo seemed cold in comparison. Lonely and sterile. Not exactly a place he'd ever wanted to rush home to.

Before he realized what he was doing, he imagined what it would be like to have a place in Christmas Bay. A place to come when he needed to feel centered, like the way Jill felt in yoga.

He smiled, sitting there, staring into the fire, lost for a moment to the rest of the world.

"Ian?"

He looked over at the sound of a voice beside him. It was low and soft, just like he remembered.

And there, standing close, was his aunt. His heartbeat slowed. He felt the heavy drum of it in his ears.

It was like he was a boy again, looking at her. Her face, more lined now and different, was still very pretty. She still looked like herself, still sounded like herself. And as she smiled, he felt like he was home again. He actually felt like he was home.

"Aunt Betty?"

Slowly, he stood. Unlike some of the other residents here, she wasn't using a walker, or even a cane. She looked frailer than when he'd seen her last, but of course she would. It had been years, and she was in her late seventies now.

"Ian," she said again, her voice cracking. She stepped closer and gazed up at him. Then she reached up and cupped his cheek in her hand. Her skin was soft, papery. He remembered that she'd done this on the day he'd come to live with her, self-exiled from Frances's house. She'd touched his face, and he'd ducked away, not wanting to be touched at all. Not wanting to be reached, even in the simplest physical sense.

"You're actually here," she said. And that was like a thousand knives being plunged into his chest. She'd always been kind to him. Even now, after he'd disappeared and had stayed gone all these years, she was still being kind to him. He didn't deserve it. He didn't deserve her.

"I am," he said. "Why don't we sit down?"

He took her elbow, although he could tell she didn't need to be helped, and guided her toward the couch.

They sat, turning so they were facing each other. Again, he felt the comforting warmth of the fire against his skin.

"What are you doing here?" she asked with a frown, worry etched over her soft features. "Is everything okay?"

"Everything is fine. It's kind of a long story, but everything is fine."

She leaned back, staring at him like he might vanish. She kept a shaky hand on his thigh, as if this would keep him grounded beside her.

"I've got time for long stories, sweetheart," she said. "If you do."

He leaned back, too. For the first time in a long while, he felt like he wanted to take his time with something. Not rush through it in order to get to the next thing on his plate. She deserved an explanation, and that was putting it mildly. The problem was, he didn't even know where to begin. His chest felt tight, his head swimmy. He could feel the receptionist, Katie, watching curiously from across the room.

He swallowed hard and looked down at his aunt's hand. Wrinkly and spotted. Her nails were painted a delicate pink. How was he supposed to explain away his absence in her life? After what she'd done for him? Now that he was an adult, he realized how much his coming to live with her must have turned her existence upside down. And he'd been such a shit. Really, there was no other way to put it.

He thought about Frances then, and how she'd done the same thing for him. And not just for him, for countless other kids who'd needed her love and care over the years. They'd all turned her existence upside down. Some, more than others.

Forcing a deep breath, he wondered if his aunt's forgiving nature would extend past this initial reunion in the lobby of her retirement home. When she knew the whole story, would she care to have anything to do with him? He wasn't sure he'd have anything to do with himself if the tables were turned.

"I should start by apologizing," he said. "But I'm not that sure I can apologize enough for not calling or visiting after I left here."

She continued watching him, patting his thigh with that slightly shaking hand. "I hoped you would call. But I'm not surprised you didn't."

"You say that like it's okay."

"You had a painful upbringing, Ian. You'd been abused for a long time before I got you. I never expected to magically fix those things. I knew you might never open up to me, or anyone else while you were here. But I needed to try."

He nodded at that. She did try. She'd tried harder than most people in his life had, except maybe Frances. Again, there was that now familiar flash of anger at himself for not seeing what had been right in front of his eyes. A home, a loving home, that he'd just discarded like a gum wrapper in the trash.

He'd never looked back. But that wasn't quite true, was it? It was more like he'd *tried* not to look back. He'd spent his adult life going from one deal to the next, trying his damnedest not to look in the rearview mirror, because if he looked too hard or too long, he'd have to face what he'd left behind. A home of his own. And then it couldn't be his mother's fault anymore. It was his.

He put his hand over hers.

"I've been trying to figure myself out," he said. "Trying to understand the choices I've made. It's true that I had a terrible childhood, but a lot of people have terrible childhoods and they don't turn their backs on the people who care about them." He thought of Stella when he said this. And Marley and Kyla. They'd been strong enough to overcome their pain. He'd let his pain overcome him. It was a real come-to-Jesus moment.

"You never turned your back on me," his aunt said. "If you had, you wouldn't be sitting here now. I'm grateful that you found your way back. I'm choosing to be grateful for that."

"You're not angry? How can you not be angry with me?"

"Because I know what kind of person you are. You always tried so hard to act like you didn't care, but you did. You do. Obviously. How could I be angry at that? It took how long it took, but here you are."

Yes. Here he was.

"I'd love to believe that you came back just for me," she continued. "But I have a feeling there's more to it than that."

She might've changed physically, but she was still sharp as a tack. She was right. There was much more to it.

"I'm a real estate developer," he said. "I live in San Francisco, but I heard that Frances O'Hara's house was going to be coming on the market soon."

She nodded slowly. "Frances O'Hara. Your foster mother..."

"Yes."

"So, you'd obviously know how valuable that property is."

"I do."

She frowned. "I'm surprised she'd want to sell

to a developer. Hasn't that house been in her family for generations?"

"It has. And she doesn't want to sell to a developer. She wants to sell it to someone who will raise a family there, like she did. She doesn't want to move, but she's got Alzheimer's and can't take care of it anymore."

His aunt appeared to let that settle. Maybe sensing what was coming next. That he'd sensed a good deal, and had come running. It didn't make him look like a very nice guy. In fact, it made him look like a grade A jackass, but it was the truth, and he was done sugarcoating the truth.

"I see," she said. "And do you have a family?"

This was the hard part. He wanted to squirm, but instead, he forced himself to sit very still. His penance.

"No. In fact, I've never been interested in that kind of life. Or, at least, I thought I wasn't. When I came up here it was for the property. I was going to tell her what she wanted to hear in order to get it. But I've spent some time with her over the last week, and I've spent some time with the other foster kids who lived there when I did, and I don't feel the same anymore..."

"You don't want to buy it?"

"If I did, I'd do it privately, not through the company. Not to develop."

She smiled. "It's a lovely house, Ian."

"I know."

"So, you might be moving back to Christmas Bay, then."

"My life is in the Bay Area, my work. I'd be lying if I said I haven't been thinking about it, though. Wondering what it would look like to spend part of the year up here. I've been in the fast lane for a long time, and I didn't know what it felt like to slow down, to *really* slow down, until I came back."

His aunt chuckled at that. "Yes, it's slower here. That's for sure."

"All that aside, I know if I don't buy this house, someone else will, and eventually it'll be sold for the property. The view alone…" He shook his head. "Well, the view alone is spectacular. Other developers will hear about it, and they'll latch on. They'll tell Frances what she wants to hear, too. And they can be relentless, believe me."

"It sounds like you've given this a lot of thought."

"I've been thinking about a lot of things," he said. "I'm not going to pretend that I'm a changed man. But the thing is, I *want* to change, and that feels like enough right now."

She leaned forward and pulled him into a hug. She smelled like baby powder and lilacs. She'd always been a hugger, and Ian had always been…well, not a hugger. He'd always avoided it, like the person doing the hugging wanted to sneakily infiltrate his defenses somehow.

But today was different. Today, he wrapped his

arms around his aunt and hugged her back. He allowed himself to feel her warmth and solidness, and to breathe in her flowery scent, and to let her take him back to the good days. There hadn't been a ton of those, but there had been some. The days she'd baked for him, or rented his favorite movies. When she'd let him back her car out of the driveway before he'd had his license. When she'd saved enough money to take him to Portland to go school shopping. An overnight trip to a nice hotel, which was his first experience outside Christmas Bay. He'd almost let himself love her then. Almost.

Now, as she pulled away, he saw that she looked close to crying. He hated himself for being something that she wished she'd done differently. He didn't want to be a regret for anyone, especially her.

"Have you been okay?" he asked quietly. "All these years?"

"I've been alright. You know what Forrest Gump says—'life is like a box of chocolates…'"

He smiled. "'You never know what you're gonna get.'"

They sat there for a long time. Talking and catching up, and before Ian knew it, they'd talked right through her lunch. Neither one of them had noticed.

They'd simply been lost to each other.

A good way to be, he thought later on. A very good way to be.

Chapter Twelve

"It's a great house," the real estate agent said, with an all-encompassing wave of her manicured hand. "Hardwood floors throughout, stackable washer and dryer, close to the pharmacy and hospital…"

Frances eyed her, and Stella could tell this last part hadn't impressed her foster mother much. She didn't want to be close to the hospital. She didn't want to be in a fifty-five and older retirement community, no matter how nice the washer and dryer was. She wanted to be in her comfortable, familiar old house above Cape Longing.

She was fairly grumpy today. She hadn't wanted to come see this place at all, but Stella and Marley had convinced her. Maybe not the best idea in retrospect…

Stella glanced over at Marley, who was bouncing the baby in her arms and looking back. They had to start looking at places, they just had to. Stella knew when they listed the house, offers would start pouring in. They needed to be ready. And at the thought of selling to anyone other than Ian, her heart sank. Again.

When, exactly, had she started wanting him to buy it? When Frances had proposed the idea of them spending time together until Christmas Eve, she couldn't wait for it to be over with. She hadn't been able to picture selling the house to Ian at all, and was going to do everything in her power to convince Frances that he was a bad seed. That anything he touched would eventually wither and wilt.

But now? Now she'd let herself hope, and hope was a very dangerous thing for someone who wasn't used to hoping for much at all. Stella was a realist, she wasn't a romantic. Yet, after talking to Loretta Dwight at the Jingle Bell Inn, she'd had the funniest feeling. It had started like a tickle in her chest, in her heart, and it had grown into a warm, insistent pulse throughout her entire body. Until she'd recognized it for what it was... *Hope*. She was hoping he'd come through for them. Despite everything. Despite her fears about being hurt. Despite overhearing him and Carter at Frances's house the other night.

She put her hands in her jacket pockets and followed the Realtor into the sunny little bedroom. How could she not start hoping, though, after hearing Loretta's story? The one where an anonymous donor had paid their hospital bill in full.

Loretta had been certain that anonymous donor had been Ian. Who else could it have been? And Stella was sure of it, too. In fact, by the time she'd climbed back in the Jeep and started the engine, she had a lump in her throat. Because *this* was what she'd meant that day—the day they'd gone to see Marley and the baby at the candy shop. They'd talked about his wealth, and she'd asked if he ever thought about helping people with it. She still remembered the look on his face. Defensive. Maybe even a little surprised that she'd asked. It had been bold, probably a little rude of her, but she'd wanted to put him in his place. She'd wanted to be right about him all along.

But the problem was, she hadn't been right about him. She'd been very, very wrong. Someone who would pay an entire hospital bill was not a jerk. That was someone who had a heart. A big one at that.

So, yes. She'd let herself hope that maybe, just maybe, he'd want the house for something other than its resale value. That he'd been sincere when he'd asked her for another chance, a chance to prove himself to her.

But that hope, that wonderful, warm pulsing feeling in her chest, had eased a bit because she hadn't been able to track him down, no matter how hard she'd tried. He hadn't answered his phone or returned her messages. He'd just…disappeared. And Christmas Eve and the Flotilla of Lights were just a few days away now.

Frowning, she watched the Realtor point out the view from the bedroom window. A perfectly nice yard, with a pretty maple tree and a small garden off to the side. But it was so far from what Frances was used to on the cape that it broke Stella's heart a little. A new view wasn't the only thing her foster mother would have to start getting used to. She was going to have to start living her life differently. Accepting help when she was so used to being an independent woman. Selling the house was symbolic for her, Stella and her foster sisters knew that. It would be so much easier if she knew the house was going to be loved by someone else. It would be so much easier to say goodbye and let it go.

Stella took a deep breath and let it out slowly. It was time to start considering the possibility that Ian wasn't going to be that person. Despite this roller coaster of events and emotions, and despite the fact that he genuinely seemed to have come to a gentler place inside himself when it came to Christmas Bay. She'd seen it happen, she'd seen it in his eyes. *Change.* But no matter how much he'd changed, he might not be ready for anything else. And that was okay. If he wasn't ready for the house, if he wasn't ready for her, she'd rather he walk away now and save everyone a lot of heartache.

She felt the sting of tears as she looked out the window, not really seeing the landscape beyond. It was a nice thought, saving everyone the heartache. But she knew her heart was going to be pummeled, anyway. It didn't matter if he disappeared now, or after Christmas Eve. Gone was gone.

"Would you mind if we talked alone for a minute?" Marley asked the Realtor with a smile. The baby had fallen asleep in the carrier strapped to her chest, and looked like a little cherub with her rosy cheeks and heart-shaped lips. She was dressed in another Christmas onesie today. The child had more clothes than Stella did.

"Of course," the Realtor said. "I'll just be in the other room if you have any questions."

Frances watched her go with her arms crossed over her chest.

"Frances," Stella said. "You don't have to pretend to like it for our sakes."

It was meant to be a joke to lighten the mood, but Frances didn't smile. She actually looked a little pouty right then. A little petulant. She didn't want to be looking at this place. But it was much more than that. It was obvious that she resented what was happening to her. Stella knew it had to be extraordinarily frustrating not to feel like you were in control of your future. It had to feel like the entire world was conspiring against you, and you were just standing on the sidelines watching it happen.

Stella walked over and put an arm around her foster mother's shoulders. She felt stiff as a board. "I'm sorry," she said. "We shouldn't have dragged you out here today. But we wanted you to start getting an idea of what's available. What you might be interested in moving into."

"Well, I don't want to be in a fifty-five and older community," Frances said with a shake of her head. "It's fine for a lot of people, but not me. I want kids riding their bikes down the street. I want families for my neighbors."

"Okay," Marley said. "I totally understand. The most important thing is that you're close to us in town. There are a lot of places to choose from. You don't have to be anywhere you don't want to be. I'm sorry if we made you feel like that. This is your decision, Frances."

Frances's shoulders slumped then. "I don't mean to seem ungrateful. I know you girls are trying to help, and it's not easy helping a stubborn old goat like me. Especially one who can't remember her own name half the time."

"Frances..." Stella rubbed her back, wishing there was something she could say to ease this transition. But the truth was, it was going to be brutal, no matter what. They just needed to get through it the best way they could.

"No, it's true," Frances said. "I'm thankful you're here with me and have taken this on. But it's so hard to leave the house. I can't explain how hard. I was really hoping that Ian would want it. I really was…"

"I know." Marley frowned, looking over at Stella. "Have you heard from him? He's still in town, right?"

It looked like Stella wasn't the only one who'd been holding out hope for Ian to come save the day.

She cleared her throat. "I'm not sure, actually. I think he's still here, but I haven't been able to reach him. He hasn't returned my calls…"

There was no doubt about it. Frances looked heartbroken at that.

"I'm sorry, Stella," Marley said quietly. She'd known from the very beginning how Stella felt about Ian. She'd been able to see beyond her foster sister's prickly exterior where he was concerned, to her softness underneath. She knew that Frances wasn't the only one heartbroken here, but for very different reasons.

Stella shrugged, trying to look like she didn't care that much. Which was ridiculous. Everyone knew she did.

"It is what it is," she said. "He probably just needs some time. I'm sure he'll be in touch." But she really didn't know for sure. She was actually worried she wouldn't hear from him again. That he'd go back to San Francisco without ever contacting her, without contacting Frances to explain his decision. And that would be the worst outcome of all. Never getting to say goodbye, or have any kind of closure for whatever had started between them.

"Hey," Marley said, suddenly sounding overly chipper. "Why don't we go get some ice cream?"

When they were kids, ice cream had cured whatever ailed them. Frances had been shameless about it. Period cramps? Ice cream would fix it. Boyfriend troubles? Ice cream. Bad grade on a test? Ice cream, ice cream, ice cream.

Stella smiled. It was impossible not to. "I could go for some rocky road. What do you say, Frances?"

"Actually, that sounds wonderful," Frances said. "Ice cream fixes everything, right?"

Maybe not *everything*. But today, it would have to do.

Ian sat in his fancy office chair, the one that had set him back three grand, and looked out over the sparkling San Francisco Bay. Sailboats cut through the water, bobbing up and down over the wintery swells. It was a beautiful morning. Clear and crisp, with a sky so blue, it almost hurt to look at it.

He set his jaw. He hadn't shaved yet. He'd come close last night, but had stopped himself at the last minute, unable or unwilling to cut that sentimental tie to Christmas Bay. He'd started growing the beard when he'd started growing a conscience.

After visiting with his aunt, he'd gone back to his motel to grab his things, and then he'd checked out. Quietly. Without seeing Loretta, the front desk lady, who'd apparently gone home for the day, but had been trying to track him down ever since he'd made that phone call to Christmas Bay General. Without seeing anyone really, which was how he'd wanted it. He knew he'd needed the time and separation from the people he'd come to care about in Christmas Bay in order to think clearly. And to do that, he needed to be back in the city, without anything influencing his thoughts or feelings.

Ian sighed, looking out over the water. He'd simply needed space to figure out how he felt, *really* felt, and to make some decisions. He didn't want to half-ass anything—he'd done too much of that already. Throwing his money and influence around, not caring who it affected, or who he might hurt in the process. He was done with that way of doing business. He was certainly done with living his life that way. Whatever decisions he made from here on out needed to be lead with his heart. It was as simple as that.

There was a soft knock on his door, and he turned to see Jill standing there, holding a stack of files.

"You've been quiet," she said. "I was just checking on you. Making sure you're okay."

"I'm fine. Come in. Sit for a second." He motioned toward the leather chair across from his desk.

She raised her brows. Ian wasn't one for idle chit-chat. At least, he'd never been interested in it as long as they'd known each other.

But now he realized that he hadn't asked Jill about

herself, or her family, or about her life in general, for a very long time.

She walked up to his desk and stood there hesitantly, still clutching the files to her chest. "You want me to…sit?"

He nodded, then smiled, to let her know he wasn't completely off his nut.

She put the files on his desk and sat on the edge of the chair. Like she expected him to change his mind at any minute.

"What's going on?" she asked. "You seem different."

"I do?" He wondered if that sounded as stupid to her as it did to him. Of course, he was different. This behavior was completely unlike him. Yet, he managed to say it with a straight face. *It's never too late for a fresh start.* His aunt had said that. Or maybe it had been Frances. He couldn't remember now. The important thing was that it was true. It was never too late.

"Yes, you do," she said. "And it's kind of freaking me out."

"Sorry."

"Does this have anything to do with the Christmas Bay deal?"

She would've heard about this around the office. Carter would have mentioned it at the very least, and word traveled fast.

"You guessed, huh?"

"Hard not to. You left as Ian Steele, and came back the Ghost of Christmas Present."

He laughed. "That's an interesting way to put it."

"It's true. You seem…mindful now. Or something like that." She sat back, looking a little more comfortable. "Want to tell me about it?"

"Nothing much to tell. I just changed my mind."

"I know you pretty well, and you don't just change your mind."

He should've realized she wouldn't buy that. She was right—she did know him well. Well enough to call him on his BS.

"Okay," he said. "Maybe I had an attack of conscience."

She nodded. "Go on."

"It just didn't turn out to be as easy as I thought. You know how it goes—we swoop in and snatch up the property, make a ton of cash in the long run. Everyone seems happy, yada yada. Except this time…"

She waited, watching him curiously.

"This time," he continued, "I stayed long enough to give a rat's ass." He shrugged. "Simple as that, I guess."

"It's not as simple as that, Ian. Caring about people is a good thing."

He looked out the window again, watching the sailboats and trying not to let those words get to him too much. It was pretty bad when someone had to point out that being a decent human being was a good thing.

"So, you know about Frances, then?" he asked.

"I know she was your foster mother. You told me bits and pieces. Carter mentioned the rest."

He nodded. "Well, I was trying to take advantage of her. Not proud of it, but that's what I was trying to do."

"But you didn't."

"No, I didn't."

"I'm proud of you."

He looked back at her. He hadn't made anyone proud in a long time. When you were a man like him, it was easy to forget what a compliment like that felt like. In fact, he'd probably convinced himself a long time ago that he didn't care about compliments like that. But he did. Turns out, he cared a lot.

Gritting his teeth, he watched her. He'd always taken Jill for granted. Someone who would field calls for him, run errands, make coffee. She was his assistant, but she was also a human being who deserved all his respect and appreciation for hanging in there with him as long as she had. Suddenly, he felt an overwhelming sense of shame for dismissing her like someone who wasn't vital to the company, when in fact, she was part of what gave the company its heartbeat. *Good God.* The self-revelations kept coming and coming, like rabbit punches to the kidneys. It was exhausting. He needed a good stiff drink, and it wasn't even midmorning yet.

"I think I might be having a midlife crisis," he said evenly.

She laughed. "What?"

"I'm serious. Or an identity crisis or *some* kind of crisis."

"Maybe that's not such a bad thing."

"Because I'm an asshole, right?"

"I didn't say that."

"But you were thinking it."

She sighed. "Ian, you're not an asshole. I think you *try* to be. In fact, I think you've spent a lot of time perfecting that persona. But it's not who you are. A guy with a healthy ego? Nobody's arguing with that." She smiled. "But not a bad guy."

He stared at her.

"So," she continued. "Are you having a midlife crisis? I doubt it. It sounds like you just really like this house. Maybe you don't want to bulldoze it and turn it into a bunch of condos. That seems normal to me. But I think what's really going on here is that something about Christmas Bay is making you feel like you can drop your persona, and you're not used to that. It scares you."

He let that settle. She'd pretty much hit the nail on the head. It scared the hell out of him. Because if Stella Clarke, the woman he'd begun falling in love with, could see past the persona to the guy underneath, and there wasn't enough there to love back, then what? Where would that leave him? It was the thing he'd been avoiding his entire life. Letting anyone close enough to hurt him.

But he also knew that he wouldn't be able to go back to Christmas Bay without letting her get close. He knew he was going to have to reconcile his feelings for Stella before he did anything else. Before he thought any more about the house, or his aunt, or Frances or any of it. He needed to see Stella again. And all of a sudden, his next move was as clear as if he was looking through crystal and seeing to the other side.

He glanced at his watch. He'd need to fly in and rent a car in Eugene. The drive from San Francisco would take too long, and he felt anxious now that he'd made up his mind. The clock was ticking toward Christmas Eve, and what if she wouldn't see him when he got there? He'd left without telling her where he was going, after all. He'd felt like he'd had a good reason, but hadn't bothered explaining it to anyone. He could blame his enormous ego for that. Just because he was experiencing a transition of some kind, didn't mean he'd changed overnight. *Baby steps, Steele.*

Jill frowned. "What are you thinking?"

"I'm thinking I need to get on the next flight to Eugene," he said.

"Why?"

"Because I've still got business in Christmas Bay. Just not the kind I'm used to."

"You're in a hurry," she said, "so I won't ask. But you'll tell me when you get back?"

He got up and smiled down at her. "You'll be the very *first* person I tell. And since you're so wise, I want to ask you a question."

"What's that?"

"What would you do with a century-old Victorian if you bought one today?" he asked. "And don't worry. It's not haunted."

Stella waved goodbye to the young mother and her little boy, and watched them walk out the door of the candy shop into the dusky light of early evening. The old-fashioned streetlamps had just flickered on, illuminating Main Street in a soft, yellow glow. Pine wreaths hung from each one, their festive red velvet ribbons fluttering in the breeze. the Flotilla of Lights was two days away. Christmas Eve was almost here, and Ian was gone.

Stella stood behind the counter, feeling a lump rise in her throat. It was the same lump that kept coming back again and again. So far, she hadn't given in to the urge to curl up and cry like a brokenhearted teenager, but it hadn't been easy. She *was* brokenhearted. But she was no teenager, and that was the only thing that kept her chin up now. She wasn't going to let this disappointment, this monumental sadness at how things had turned out, ruin her Christmas. After all, the most important thing was that it didn't appear that he was going to try to convince Frances to sell to him anymore. One less problem, she kept telling herself. One less thing to have to worry about. At least he'd spared Frances any more lies, and that was a good thing.

But try as she might, she couldn't convince her heart that it was enough. Because there had actually been more on the line than just the house. She'd gotten tangled up in this, too, and it hurt that he'd just walked away without the simplest goodbye. She'd come to think so much more of him than that. She'd come to love Ian Steele, God help her. And now, look. She was standing here trying not to cry. Again. This was what she got for letting herself believe in him.

Well, no more. She'd do a much better job of protecting herself from here on out, even if she had to be an ice queen to do it.

She looked around the little shop that Frances had decorated so cutely for Christmas. There were garlands and Christmas lights hung throughout, and a little tree in the window—trimmed with candy, of course. It looked so sweet and cozy that, for a second, Stella was overcome with emotion. She wished she could hit the pause button on time. With Frances still living in her house on the cape, and still able to remember most things. She wished things could stay like this forever. But of course, they couldn't. They would change, as things always did. But she was grateful for this moment. Even though it was complicated by the uncertainty of the future, she was grateful for her family, and for the love and support they always gave one another. When it was all said and done, they were very lucky this holiday season.

With a sigh, she reached for the keys underneath the cash register and walked over to lock the door. They still had a few minutes until closing, but it had been so slow for the last hour, she didn't think anyone would notice. Most people were probably home, in front of crackling fires, or watching Christmas movies. That's where Stella planned on being herself in about twenty minutes. She still needed to wrap presents, and she usually did that with *It's a Wonderful Life* playing in the background.

She locked the door and turned the sign around in the window, then flipped off the lights in front of the store, so only the lit garlands glowed softly throughout.

She headed to the back room to get her purse, but stopped at the sound of knocking on the front window.

She turned with an apologetic smile on her lips. "We're closed! Sorry—"

But that was all she could manage. Because standing there on the sidewalk, dressed in a black wool coat and a dark knit hat, was Ian. He was peering in the window with both hands, his breath fogging up the glass. When he saw her, he leaned back and smiled.

And her heart, her traitorous heart, skipped a beat. It wasn't supposed to be skipping beats at the sight of Ian. It was supposed to be appropriately frosty at the sight of him.

"Can I come in?" he mouthed.

She stood there watching him. Looking for a reason to tell him no. It wasn't hard to start listing them. For one thing, she hadn't heard from him in days. And after everything that had happened, she was at least entitled to an explanation. She deserved that much. And so did Frances.

"Stella," he said, his voice muffled through the glass. "Please?"

She waited another few seconds, then finally unlocked the door.

He stepped inside and let the door close with a tinkle of the bell mounted above it. He smelled good. Really good. He looked good, too. With his expensive, tailored coat. The only thing different now was the beard. It suited him, and Stella had to work not to stare.

She raised her chin, annoyed at herself. *Good grief.* Was this all it took? Apparently, she was a sucker for beards and never knew it.

"What do you want, Ian?" she said in a clipped tone. "I was just getting ready to go home."

"I know. I'm sorry. I tried getting here sooner, but I had trouble getting a rental car at the airport."

She leaned sideways to see around him. Sure

enough, there was a small Ford something or other parked at the curb. So, he'd gone back to the city. He *had* left without saying goodbye. She'd guessed it, of course, but the reality was still hard to swallow. The question was, why in the world had he come back?

"I know you're upset," he said, swiping his hat off. It left his dark hair sticking up in the back. She prayed she could get through this interaction without launching herself into his arms. Because despite everything, he was a sight for sore eyes.

Remember, she thought. *Ice queen!*

She crossed her arms over her chest, just so she had something to do with them. "Why wouldn't I be upset?" she asked. "You just disappeared."

"I know. And I'm sorry about that. But I had to leave to get some perspective. And I've never been good at this kind of thing…"

"Communication?"

"Not when I'm emotionally involved." He shrugged. "I'll admit, I'm crap at it. I'm learning as I go."

She wasn't going to let that sway her. She just wasn't. "You could've called me back, Ian."

"I know. But I knew if I did, that would've clouded my judgment, and I didn't want that. I needed to make some decisions with a clear head."

"You could've texted."

"You're right. I wish I had a better excuse, but maybe part of me was seeing if I could just walk away and not look back. That's what I've always done when things have gotten complicated in my life. I move on…"

"But you came back."

"I came back."

"Why?"

"Because I couldn't leave you like that. I couldn't leave Frances, or even Christmas Bay like that."

She shook her head, taking a step backward. "Am I supposed to believe you care about us now? Just like that?"

"No," he said quietly. "Not just like that. I've always cared about you, Stella. It just took me this long to realize it. It took coming back here to open my eyes to things that I've refused to see for years."

She took another step back until her butt touched the counter. Against her better judgment, she looked up at him. His face was bathed in shadow and light from the garlands. He looked so handsome that her stomach dipped. It wasn't fair that he was this good-looking, *and* this charming, *and* this convincing. No wonder he was so successful. People simply couldn't resist him. She'd known that from the start.

And that might've been her a few days ago, but it wasn't her now. She was glad that he'd left and hadn't thought to text, or even leave a voicemail. Because it was the perfect reminder to be savvier where Ian was concerned. She was going to be smarter than she'd been a few days ago, when he was kissing her, and telling her things she wanted to hear, and giving her Elvis key chains that melted her heart.

"I went to see my aunt," he said quietly. "I wanted you to know."

She gazed up at him. And despite the vow she'd just made to herself to be more Ian savvy, she felt herself warm at that.

"You did?"

He nodded.

"And how did that go?"

He ran a hand through his hair. "She's a nice lady, so she didn't make me feel like garbage for being gone all this time. But I felt like garbage, anyway. She's gotten older, but she looks good. I think she's about as happy as she can be there. I'm relieved about that."

"I'm sure she was glad to see you."

"She was. She was very glad." He frowned, looking down at the hat in his hands. "I never should've stayed away this long."

"But you came back," she said again. And wondered when it was that she'd decided to make him feel better about leaving in the first place. She guessed she couldn't help it. He just had that effect. "You know what Frances says, it's never too late for a fresh start…"

He looked up, and suddenly his eyes were warmer. Darker. "She does say that, doesn't she?"

Stella nodded, realizing that if she was going to

live her life by this mantra, she'd be giving him another chance. Frances was wise, but she wasn't *always* right. Still, something about the words were wiggling their way into her consciousness as she stood there taking him in.

"So," he said. "Christmas Eve is day after tomorrow. I don't have much time to convince you that I'm a decent guy."

She licked her lips. "Are you still trying to convince us that you want the house, too?"

"Right now I just want you to look at me the way you looked at me last week."

"And how's that?"

He stepped forward, until he was close enough to touch. Until she could feel his warmth from where she stood. How she longed to give in to whatever this was that was happening inside her. She wanted him to rest his hand on her hip and pull her gently toward him. She wanted to kiss him again. She wanted to *be* kissed again.

But the truth was, Ian was a risky bet. As much as she was drawn to him, she also felt compelled to fight it, and there was good reason for that. She still didn't trust that he wouldn't hurt her in the end.

"Ian…" she began. Not knowing exactly what she wanted to say. Maybe trying to buy some time before he said something sweet. Or something funny. Or something infinitely charming, that would make her forget how smart she was supposed to be when it came to those charms.

He reached out and ran his knuckles down her cheek. So lightly that it felt like butterfly wings against her skin. "Stella…"

She felt herself swaying on her feet. He had a way of looking at her as if she was the most beautiful woman in the world. As if there'd never been any walls between them at all. She remembered when he'd first come to Frances's house as a teenager. She and Marley and Kyla all had secret crushes on him in the beginning. But Stella had immediately felt inferior to him back then. She'd always been embarrassed of her weight, which, looking back now, hadn't even been a thing. But her insecurities went deeper than just her physical appearance. They'd come from years and years of being torn down by her mother, until she felt ugly, stupid and unworthy of love and attention from anyone. Especially from someone who'd looked and acted like Ian. He'd acted superior, so to her, he'd simply *been* superior.

But then a wonderful thing happened. She'd started building defenses. She'd started being able to push people out and keep them out. She'd been able to protect herself, and it had been wonderful for a while, being safe and secure in her little cocoon. She let less and less people in, until she took that road trip by herself and did nothing but think about her childhood, and her life, and how much she'd let her mother's cruelty dictate how she'd been living it so far.

So, she'd started seeing those old defenses in a different light. Built to keep her lonely, even though she was rarely alone anymore. Living with Frances these last few months and helping her in the shop had been good for her. It had given her a deeper purpose, a deeper meaning to her life.

And then Ian had shown up. And the defenses that she'd tried to dismantle a little went right back up again. It was an epic battle of wills. Stella vs. Stella.

But as she gazed up at him now, with her walls crumbling for the second time in a matter of weeks, she was tired of analyzing it all. She wanted to feel, not just wonder what feeling would be like. She was acutely aware that pain might come with the joy, but she was so desperate for the joy that, right then, she couldn't bring herself to be afraid of that possibility anymore. She just wanted to step closer to Ian, and let him wrap her in his arms, and not think so much about it. *Ice queen be damned...*

"It seems like I've been waiting my entire life to come back here," he said quietly. "But I never recognized that feeling for what it was."

She watched him. How his brows were furrowed, just a little. Like the revelation was profound.

"I know exactly what you mean," she said.

"You do?"

She nodded. "It's like it was meant to be."

"The problem is, I've never believed in destiny before."

"Maybe it's not destiny. Maybe it's just home..."

He smiled slowly. His gaze was warm and heavy, his scent making her toes curl. She loved how that word felt coming from her lips just now. *Home.*

"Do you want to take a walk with me?" he asked.

"Now?"

"Right now. I've never walked down Main Street to see the lights before."

"Never?"

"Never."

She smiled back.

There was a first time for everything.

Chapter Thirteen

Ian walked beside Stella, their footsteps making a gentle cadence on the sidewalk. There weren't very many people out. He guessed the chilly fog that had rolled in from the beach in the last half hour put a damper on the whole being outside thing. Even if it was Christmas.

He didn't mind. In fact, he'd always liked the fog. The way it shrouded everything and made it look misty and dreamlike. That was especially true tonight, with the Christmas lights outlining the shop windows, and the soft streetlamps leading them down the sidewalk, cutting a glowing path through the haze. Christmas Bay was known for its beauty, but he didn't think it had ever looked more beautiful.

He buried his hands farther into his jacket pockets, his elbow bumping against Stella's. What he really wanted was to put his arm around her, but he was trying to give her space. He was trying not to push, to let her come to her own conclusions about their relationship. Whatever that was.

But not putting his arm around her was turning out to be one of the hardest things he'd ever done. Second only to not kissing her back there in the candy shop.

"Have you ever been in love before?" she asked, startling him from his thoughts. From the sound of their footsteps on the pavement.

He looked over at her, but she continued staring straight ahead. Like she might be afraid to look at him.

It seemed like a simple question. And he guessed for most people it would be. Most *normal* people had been in love at least once by the time they reached their thirties. But Ian had never been what he'd consider normal. He was emotionally stunted, if he was being honest with himself. He didn't think he'd been in love, truly in love, in his entire life. And why? Because he simply hadn't allowed it. Love was messy. It rarely followed any rules. It came and it did what it wanted, and then it left without warning. Ian had never been a huge fan of love. It was too damn fickle.

"Have I ever been in love…?" he muttered. "I'm going to have to say, no. I haven't."

She did glance over then. Her eyes were so dark in the mist. Her hair, damp and curling past her shoulders. The tip of her nose was red in the cold night air, and her freckles stood out all over her cheeks. She was so pretty.

"Never?"

He pretended to think, then shook his head. "Nope, never."

"Have you ever come close?"

"Yes, I think so. But my version of coming close and your version are probably different."

"You might be surprised." She was quiet for a minute. Then she took an audible breath. "Why do you think you haven't been in love before?"

"Because I've always loved myself too much to pay much attention to anyone else."

She smiled at that. "At least you're being honest."

"I told you. I'm not going to lie to you anymore."

She kicked at a pebble with the toe of her shoe.

"What about you?" he asked. "Have you been in love?"

"That's a hard question."

"Either you have or you haven't."

"I think I wanted to be in love. And, like you, I think I've come close. But I don't think I've ever really trusted anyone to love me back, and that's a problem."

"Yeah," he said. "Reciprocation would be nice."

"I don't know. I think what I need is some kind of over-the-top declaration or something. I'm a tough nut to crack. Hard to convince, you know how it goes."

"You? *Nah.*"

She laughed. "Are you saying I'm stubborn?"

"Yes, Stella. I'm saying you're stubborn. Almost as stubborn as I am."

"Did we know this back when we were kids?" She asked. "That we were meeting our matches all those years ago?"

"Hardly. But I did know I was in the presence of someone special. I was a dumb kid, but I knew that part well enough."

"Well..." She let her voice trail off. It was possible that he'd embarrassed her. Her cheeks were pink, but that could've been from the cold.

He cleared his throat. "I guess asking if you've been in love before isn't the question I really want an answer to..."

She looked over again and raised her brows.

"What I really want to know is...are you in love now?"

She slowed, then came to a stop and turned to face him. "What?"

He stopped, too. He could hardly believe he'd just asked her that. But the words were out now and hanging in the air, and it was too late to suck them back in. It was like one of those weird dreams where you didn't know you were dreaming, and your heart was pounding, and your head was swimming, and everything felt surreal.

"Because when I told you I hadn't been in love before," he said, "I meant, *before*, before." He swallowed hard, as she gazed up at him with those denim-blue eyes. A strand of Christmas lights twinkled in a storefront window a few yards away, and her face was lit up with it. "Before us," he finished evenly.

Her mouth was open slightly, and her lips were full and glistening. The mist clung to her hair and lashes, making them dark and spiky. He'd thought she was pretty before, but he'd been wrong. She was possibly the most beautiful person, inside and out, that he'd ever met in his life. She was tough and sweet, she was loyal and bold. She was smart and wild and tender and compassionate. She was the entire package, and she was standing there now with an answer teetering on those kissable lips.

He'd opened himself up to this. He had nobody to blame but himself if she pushed him away. But he was so tired of denying himself the things he wanted most in life. Or worse, convincing himself he didn't need them in the first place. But who didn't need to love? Who didn't need to be loved in return? It was a basic human emotion that Ian had gone without for so long that he'd ended up carving a hollow spot inside himself that had grown and grown, and now it was cavernous. Empty and cold and lonely.

He wanted to change his life. He *needed* to change his life. And he had to put himself out there to do it.

"Are you asking me if I love you, Ian?" she asked, her voice impossibly soft.

His neck heated. His chest felt like it was going to crack wide open, and all his emotions, all his insecurities and fears, would spill out onto the sidewalk at their feet. What a mess that would be.

He clenched his jaw and stared down at her. He'd told her he wouldn't lie to her again. And meant it.

"Yes," he said. "That's what I'm asking."

The expression on her face relaxed. He thought he could smell her perfume right then. Something light and floral. It reminded him of being young, with his whole life ahead of him. Back then he couldn't wait to leave this town and everyone in it behind. He wished he could go back and explain to himself that leaving wasn't going to solve anything. But he couldn't do that. All he could do was try to be gentle with that boy inside him.

"Then I'll tell you the truth," Stella said slowly. "I think I've always loved you. From the first time I saw you. I tried not to, but I did."

It was hard to believe what he'd just heard. But the more people who told him they cared about him, the more he was going to have to trust them. No more walls.

His heart swelled as he reached up and cradled her face with both hands. Despite the cold, her cheeks were warm. Her eyes were warm. "Would you believe me if I told you the same thing?" he asked.

She gazed up at him. "You know that's going to be hard for me…"

He smiled. "Because you need a big declaration?"

"Tough nut to crack…"

"Would you settle for a kiss? Until I can think of something better?"

"I guess I—"

He didn't give her time to finish. He leaned down and pressed his lips to hers. Tasting her, loving her.

He knew if he turned around right then, he'd be able to see Frances's house on the hill in the distance. Its Christmas lights cutting through the fog, like beacons in the night. That house, and all the love inside it, had led him home again.

Stella stood on her tiptoes and wrapped her arms around his neck. He could feel the softness of her body through her jacket. The swell of her breasts, the curve of her back. He could smell the shampoo in her hair and the soap on her skin.

She had infiltrated his senses. She'd infiltrated his heart.

Stella put the Jeep into Park the next evening, and turned off the engine.

"He said he wanted us here at six?" This, from Frances, who was in the passenger's seat beside her.

Marley and Kyla were in the back, the baby sleeping soundly in her car seat between them.

Stella picked up her phone and brought up the text from Owen that she'd gotten that morning.

Six sharp! Don't be late!

"That's what he said." She set the phone in the console and twisted around to look at her foster sisters in the darkness of the cab. The lights were on in the Tiger Sharks parking lot, but they were few and far between. She could barely see their faces clearly. "Marley, do you have any idea what this is about?"

Marley shrugged. "He wouldn't tell me. And I threatened him with no sex for a month, so I know it's serious."

"Kyla?"

"I think Ben might know, but he's being tight-lipped, too. It's exasperating."

Stella chewed her bottom lip, considering this.

"Nothing to do but go in and find out," Frances said, unbuckling her seat belt. "Unless you want me to stay here with the baby, Marley?"

"It's okay, Frances," Marley said. "I'll bring her with us. Once she's asleep, a sonic boom wouldn't wake her."

They all stepped out of the Jeep and into the cold night air. Stella had a tight feeling in her stomach, and butterflies were bumping around against her rib cage, but she couldn't understand why. Owen was always doing things like this. It was probably a Christmas surprise for Marley. Something sweet and romantic that he wanted to share with the whole family. It was exactly something he would do.

Marley tucked a soft quilt around Emily and hooked the car seat over her arm.

"Owen's pulling out all the stops for you, Marls," Stella said, closing the Jeep's door after her.

"Who says this has anything to do with me?"

Stella let that settle for a second, then followed

her family through the front gates of the ballpark and looked around. The stadium lights had just blinked on and were now blazing through the night.

She shivered and pulled her jacket collar up around her neck. What in the world was Owen up to?

"Merry Christmas!" a voice boomed over the loud-speakers.

Stella jumped. Frances laughed, delighted. The baby didn't even open her eyes. Marley was right—she was out like a light.

That had definitely been Owen's voice. Stella looked over at Marley, who just shrugged in response.

Stella narrowed her eyes at her. She was starting to think her foster sisters knew more about this than they were letting on. For one thing, Marley couldn't seem to stop *smiling*. For another, she kept leaning toward Kyla and whispering things Stella obviously wasn't supposed to hear.

"Stop by the concession stand for some peppermint hot chocolate," Owen said over the loudspeakers. "And then take your seats behind home plate. Best seats in the house!"

Frances clapped her mittened hands together. "Oh, this is wonderful!"

"Frances," Stella said, hooking her arm in her foster mother's. "Are you *sure* you don't know what this is all about?"

"Not a clue, honey. But I love surprises, don't you?"

She wasn't sure. She'd never really been surprised before.

They all headed toward the concession stand, which was empty, of course. But there were four steaming cups of hot cocoa on the counter, complete with marshmallows.

Stella's stomach curled into a warm little ball at the sight. Peppermint hot chocolate. Her *absolute* favorite. Not many people knew that. Marley, Kyla and Frances, of course. But she'd told Ian the night of Gracie's Christmas pageant. They'd been talking about comfort foods, and they'd both listed hot chocolate as a seasonal favorite. Stella had been surprised— Ian seemed more like an espresso kind of guy. But there were a lot of things about Ian that were turning out to be a surprise.

Kyla, Marley and Frances all stepped forward to take their hot cocoa, then turned to look back at her.

"Coming," she murmured. "I'm coming."

She picked up her own cup and breathed in the rich, familiar scent. Then she took a sip, careful not to burn her tongue.

"Oh, my God," Kyla said, licking the melted marshmallow off her top lip. "There's no way this is ballpark hot chocolate. This is delicious."

Marley took a sip, too. "Nope. It's ballpark, alright."

Stella smiled. Her foster sister knew her concession stand foods and drinks. She was the Tiger Sharks announcer, after all. Not to mention living with their head coach.

"Okay, guys," she said. "*What* is going on, here?"

Marley winked at her. "Only one way to find out. Come on."

Now, she knew for sure something was up. Both of her foster sisters were smiling. Grinning from ear to ear, was more like it. Frances was the only other person who seemed to be in the dark with Stella, and she looked like a little kid right then. Enchanted by the mystery and magic of it all.

They all headed to the bleachers behind home plate, clutching their hot chocolate and chattering excitedly. Except for Stella. She kept looking around for someone in particular, but she didn't want to admit, even to herself, who she was looking for.

But really, there was no use. She'd fallen so hard that she'd probably always be looking for Ian now. Hoping to see him around every corner in Christmas Bay. In every storefront, and every little café. He'd come back to town and had wrapped himself around their lives like a warm blanket. She wasn't sure how she'd ever do without him now.

She climbed up on the bleachers and sat in between Frances and the baby in her car seat. Leaning down, she kissed Emily's downy little head, careful not to disturb her. She looked so cozy underneath her quilt that she reminded Stella of a cherub right then. All rosy cheeks and pouty lips, and soft, curling hair.

Stella's heart squeezed. Maybe someday she'd have a baby of her own. She'd never really let herself want that before. But something about tonight, about this Christmas in particular, was making her consider things that had seemed far away before. Unattainable. Or at the very least, unlikely.

But a family of her own didn't have to be an unlikely concept. Why couldn't she have a baby someday? Just because she'd had a hard childhood, and hadn't been loved like she should have been by her parents, didn't mean she hadn't been loved at all. She'd found love with Frances. She'd found happiness with Frances. And now, she'd found happiness with Ian, too. Sure, it might be fleeting. But she'd take it. There was enough love and happiness to go around. That's what this holiday season had taught her so far.

"It this thing on?"

She looked up, startled from her thoughts. And saw Ian standing on the pitcher's mound, holding a microphone. He was smiling, tapping it for effect.

Her foster sisters gasped. Frances scooted forward on the bleachers, as if she'd miss something if she wasn't a few inches closer.

Stella's heart beat warm and heavy inside her chest. She was afraid to blink, for fear the image of Ian under the bright stadium lights would disappear. That *he* would disappear, and she'd find out that she'd been dreaming this all along.

But finally, she did blink. And he didn't disappear. In fact, he locked gazes with her and grinned wide. His new beard brought out his eyes, which were so blue that she knew they'd break her heart up close. He wore his dark wool coat and a red scarf. He looked like he'd just stepped out of a Christmas movie, with his handsome, movie-star smile.

"It pays to know the Tiger Sharks head coach," he said into the microphone. "When you need an entire ballpark to make a statement, that is."

Stella laughed, then felt tears threaten and waved her hand in front of her face to cut the vapors, an old Frances trick.

"Stella," he continued, "you said you needed a big declaration. So, here's the cheesiest thing I could think of. Because if completely embarrassing myself in front of your family doesn't convince you that I'm in love with you, I don't know what will."

Kyla and Marley looked over at her and smiled. Their eyes were glassy. She wasn't the only one struggling not to cry.

Frances put a hand on her knee and squeezed. "Oh, honey," she said softly.

"So," Ian said, "here goes…"

There was a pause, the sound of him breathing nervously into the microphone, and then music started playing.

Stella let out a long breath that she hadn't realized she'd been holding. "Love Me Tender," her favorite

Elvis song ever written, started rippling out over the loudspeakers like a long, dark ribbon. And then Ian began singing the words. Terribly.

She smiled and put a hand over her mouth. He was tone-deaf, and he was stumbling hopelessly over the lyrics. But it was the most wonderful, most romantic thing that anyone had ever done for her.

Next to her, Frances was straight-up crying. The baby slept, unaware that this amazing, whimsical thing was happening right in front of her. Stella knew she'd be telling her about it when she was older. A teenager, maybe, when she'd appreciate the sheer romance of it all. Or when her own heart had been stolen by a handsome young man willing to do any-thing and everything in his power to show her that he loved her.

Stella sat there clutching her chest, watching him sing. And then he sang the very last line and lowered the microphone to his side.

She cupped her hands around her mouth. "Bravo!" she shouted, her voice hitching a little. "Bravo!"

Her foster sisters were on their feet, clapping and whistling. Their breath forming clouds on the cold night air.

Ian bent over and laid the microphone down on the pitching mound. Then he made his way toward them, his ocean-blue gaze locked on Stella's. Her heart, which she'd been trying so hard to protect over these last few weeks, was his. There was no other way to put it. She was 100 percent, hopelessly in love.

He smiled as he approached. She could smell his aftershave on the breeze as he got closer. Her stomach curled like it did every time she was in his presence. Only now, she knew he felt the same way. It was a wonderful feeling, to love and be loved in return. It was the most wonderful feeling in the world.

"Well?" he asked, coming to a stop in front of her and her family. "How'd I do?"

How'd I do? Stella considered this. There really weren't enough words. He'd managed to change in the short amount of time that he'd been here. He'd grown vulnerable, despite his past. He'd chosen to be open and honest and raw, even if it meant he could be hurt in the end. She could see this written all over his face, and it did something to her. It made her want to be just as open, just as raw. If Ian could do it, so could she.

"If I weren't already engaged," Kyla said, "I'd marry you."

Frances stepped forward and wrapped her arms around his waist, resting her head against his chest. He hugged her back. Tightly, and with no hesitation.

"Frances," he said. "I need to talk to you about your house. I need to—"

"Shh," she said, pulling away to look up at him. "The house isn't the most important thing. Family is what's most important to me. It always has been."

He smiled, and there was something in his eyes

that said he wasn't done with the subject yet, but he'd let it go for now. For now, they'd just enjoy the moment.

Frances stepped away, and Ian's gaze shifted to Stella. Her pulse fluttered behind her ears. She simply couldn't believe there were happy endings like this in the world. She'd been so used to her story being a little worn around the edges. A little sad and a little too real. But here she was, looking up at a man who'd just sung to her. *Badly.* In an empty baseball stadium, with her family there as witnesses. Really, could it get any better than this?

"What about you?" he asked, his voice so low that she knew, in the end, this was for her and her alone. Not to prove anything, not to have other people see and help convince her of something. It was simply a way of showing her how he felt. Truly felt, deep down.

She stepped forward, her legs trembling.

He stepped forward, too, until she could feel his incredible warmth. Until, finally, he was pressed close, and his arms were wrapped around her.

She tilted her head back and smiled. "That was quite a declaration."

"You said you needed one."

"And you delivered."

He nodded, watching her. "I'm not saying I'm perfect, Stella. There are still a lot of things I need to work through. Things I need to fix. But being here, being here with you, it's a start."

A lovely heat bloomed across her chest, up her neck, and onto her cheeks. She could feel her heart skipping, just like a teenager's. She thought about that insecure little girl she'd been. The one who wore T-shirts and shorts instead of bathing suits in the summer. The one who thought she'd never seen anyone as beautiful as Ian Steele, and never dreamed that he'd see her as beautiful, too. As a girl that he could love. She guessed that's what life was all about. Growing up enough to prove yourself wrong.

She'd been wrong about Ian. She'd been wrong about herself.

"It's never too late for a fresh start," she said softly.

"No," he said, leaning close. "It isn't."

And then he kissed her. Long and slow, until she forgot about everything but how he made her feel.

Loved.

Epilogue

Ian had seen a lot of beautiful things in his life. The Eiffel Tower on Valentine's Day, the Grand Canyon during a burning July sunset. Venice, where the gondolas slid through the water like ancient creatures, the lights of the city reflected in the darkness of the midnight currents.

But he didn't think he'd ever seen anything as gorgeous as the Flotilla of Lights on Christmas Eve.

He stood there now, on the steep, rocky banks of the bay, watching the fishing boats make their way through the fog, the lanterns strung across their bows like stars.

Stella stood close beside him, tucked into his side like she was always meant to be there. Frances stood on his other side, along with Kyla, Ben and Gracie.

And then Marley, Owen and the baby, who really wasn't a baby anymore. Emily had just celebrated her second birthday, and was now a wriggly, chubby-faced toddler. She giggled as Owen bounced her on his hip and made motorboat sounds with his lips. An Emily favorite.

Ian smiled. She was pretty damn cute, and by this point, he'd hung out with his fair share of kids. Of course, the kids that he spent time with were teenagers, but still. They'd been toddlers once, too.

Leaning down, he nuzzled Stella behind her ear, breathing her in. She closed her eyes and sighed contentedly. Two years ago, he would've been hard-pressed to believe he could end up this happy. That Frances would actually accept his offer on her house, but she had. She'd trusted him with her heart, signed on the dotted line, and for once in his life, Ian had come through.

Now, for two weeks out of the year, the house on Cape Longing was a summer camp for kids in the foster system. Kids who'd been shuffled around their entire lives and were just now learning how special they were. That they were loved. And that home could look like a lot of different things to a lot of different people.

Ian still spent a good amount of time at his office in San Francisco, but he'd also found a balance that allowed him to spend a good amount of time in Christmas Bay, too. Until now, he'd only come up for weekends and holidays, and to spend as much time with Stella as he could. But tonight, he was planning on making a shift that would mean living in the house most of the year, and working remotely. Carter had given him her blessing, and truthfully, he knew she was looking forward to running the show on her own from down there, anyway. *You'll be out of my hair!* she'd said jokingly. But of course, she hadn't really been joking.

Stella looked at her watch. "Oh, we'd better get going, babe. The concert starts at seven. It was so crowded last year..."

"Don't worry," he said. "Aunt Betty is saving seats for us."

This was the second annual Weatherly Court Christmas Concert, and it was turning into quite the to-do. The price of tickets went toward helping local families who were having a hard time paying their bills over the holidays. That had been Ian's idea. His aunt had pitched it to Weatherly's activity director, who'd then pitched it to the owner, who'd ended up loving it.

Frances had loved it, too. When he'd invited her to the concert last year and told her where the admission fees were going, she'd taken his face in her hands and gazed up at him endearingly. "I'm so happy you came home," she'd said. "Have I told you that lately?"

He looked over at her now, in her festive cap and

mittens. She told him all the time. Sometimes she remembered telling him, and sometimes she didn't. But it was fine. He liked hearing it over and over again. It reminded him that there were people here who loved him.

His heart thumped as he watched her lean over and kiss Emily on the cheek. He'd love to say that things with Frances had been easy over the last couple of years, but that wouldn't be entirely true. Her memory loss had progressed some, and the move out of the house had been tough on her. Even so, it had been immediately clear to all of them that it was the right thing to do. Moving had been the hardest part, but once she was settled into her cute little beach-front cottage, it was like a new peace had washed over her. Without the heavy decision of what to do with the house in the mix, she seemed younger now. Happier. More joyful. Even if she couldn't remember all of the details, all of the time.

Stella had taken over running the candy shop, something she was turning out to be very good at. Exceptional, really. Ian told her this often, and she'd only blush and shake her head. *I'm just happy to be helping Frances*, she'd say. But it was more than that. She had a great head for business—he'd been able to tell from the beginning. He was proud of Stella. It didn't seem like there was anything she couldn't do if she set her mind to it. And she set her mind to a lot of things. He'd been witness.

Ian put his hand in his pocket and touched the small, velvet box there. He was nervous, but that was okay. The nervousness was just proof this meant something. Actually, the truth was, it meant everything.

"Stella," he said softly.

She turned away from the boats gliding through the fog and looked up at him. Her eyes were beautiful. Dark and deep. Full of love. Love for him. He was so thankful he'd come back here, to this town where he'd grown up. It had been a rough journey, there was no denying that. But the destination had been worth it all.

"I love you," he said.

She smiled. "I love you, too, baby."

Slowly, he pulled the little box from his pocket. So small, yet so significant. He felt like he was holding his entire future in his hand. If she'd just say yes, he thought their happiness might be immeasurable. Corny, maybe. But true.

"You like declarations," he said, leaning down to give her a soft kiss on the temple. "And I know you love Christmas Eve, so I've been waiting for tonight…"

She looked down at his hand, and her eyes widened. Her heart-shaped mouth opened slightly, and she exhaled into the cold night air.

"Ian," she said. "Is that…"

He could sense the rest of the family watching now. In quiet excitement and anticipation. This was exactly how it should be. Because they were his family, too.

"Merry Christmas," he said.

She didn't say anything. But as it turned out, she didn't have to.

She simply reached up and wrapped her arms around his neck. Kissed his lips like she'd done a thousand times before. But this would never get old. Because this was Stella who was kissing him. His Stella.

And he was hers.

* * * * *

Catch up with the previous titles in
Kaylie Newell's new Harlequin Special Edition
miniseries Sisters of Christmas Bay

Their Sweet Coastal Reunion
Their All-Star Summer

Available now!

HARLEQUIN
PLUS

Try the best multimedia subscription service for romance readers like you!

Read, Watch and Play.

Experience the easiest way to get the romance content you crave.

Start your **FREE TRIAL** at
<u>www.harlequinplus.com/freetrial</u>.